John Godfrey Saxe

The Money King

John Godfrey Saxe

The Money King

ISBN/EAN: 9783743312340

Manufactured in Europe, USA, Canada, Australia, Japa

Cover: Foto ©Andreas Hilbeck / pixelio.de

Manufactured and distributed by brebook publishing software
(www.brebook.com)

John Godfrey Saxe

The Money King

THE

MONEY-KING

AND

OTHER POEMS.

BY

JOHN G. SAXE.

BOSTON:
TICKNOR AND FIELDS.
M DCCC LX.

RIVERSIDE, CAMBRIDGE:

STEREOTYPED AND PRINTED BY

H. O. HOUGHTON AND COMPANY.

To Mrs. George P. Marsh:

A Lady endowed with the best Gifts of Nature and Culture, and adorned with all Womanly Graces, — this volume is inscribed by her Friend,

The Author.

PREFACE.

————◆————

ABOUT ten years ago, at the instance of my friend,
JAMES T. FIELDS, Esq., and with much misgiving, I
ventured on the publication of a volume of poems.
For the favor it has found with the public, — as
evinced in a demand for sixteen editions of the book;
and with the critics, — as shown in many kind and
scholarly reviews, — I take this occasion to express
my grateful acknowledgments. Of the little which I
have written since the first publication of that volume, the
greater part will be found in this. In the arrangement
of my materials, I have put "The Money-King" in
front, simply on account of its length; as, in military
usage, the tallest soldier is commonly placed at the
head of the file. For the two episodes which inter-
rupt the thread of this otherwise consecutive perform-
ance, I must plead the authority of greater names,
ancient and modern. The poem entitled "The Way
of the World," is little more than a paraphrase of a

passage in a prose story lately published in Frazer's Magazine; and the plot of the Chinese Tale is mainly borrowed from an extremely clever English book, entitled " The Porcelain Tower." The rest of the pieces, for aught I can say, are as original as the verses of other men who have the misfortune to write at this rather late period in the history of letters; but if (as may possibly happen) any expressions which I have supposed to be my own, should be found in the works of earlier writers, I can only answer, with the hearty indignation of old DONATUS : — " *Pereant isti qui ante nostra dixerunt !* "

CONTENTS.

———

THE MONEY-KING.

A POEM DELIVERED BEFORE THE PHI BETA KAPPA SOCIETY OF YALE COLLEGE 1854.

THE MONEY-KING.

As landsmen, sitting in luxurious ease,
Talk of the dangers of the stormy seas ;
As fireside travellers, with portentous mien,
Tell tales of countries they have never seen ;
As parlor-soldiers, graced with fancy-scars,
Rehearse their bravery in imagined wars ;
As arrant dunces have been known to sit
In grave discourse of wisdom and of wit ;
As paupers, gathered in congenial flocks,
Babble of banks, insurances, and stocks ;
As each is oft'nest eloquent of what
He hates or covets, but possesses. not ; —
As cowards talk of pluck ; misers, of waste ;
Scoundrels, of honor ; country-clowns, of taste ;
Ladies, of logic ; devotees, of sin ;

Topers, of water ; temperance-men, of gin ; —
I sing of MONEY ! — no ignoble theme,
But loftier far than poetasters dream,
Whose fancies, soaring to their native moon,
Rise like a bubble or a gay balloon,
Whose orb aspiring takes a heavenward flight,
Just in proportion as it's thin and light !

Kings must have Poets.   From the earliest times,
Monarchs have loved celebrity in rhymes ;
From good King *Robert*, who, in *Petrarch's* days,
Taught to mankind the proper use of bays,
And, singling out the prince of Sonneteers,
Twined wreaths of laurel 'round his blushing ears ;
Down to the Queen, who, to her chosen bard,
In annual token of her kind regard,
Sends, not alone the old poetic greens,
But, like a woman and the best of queens,
Adds to the leaves, to keep them fresh and fine,
The wholesome moisture of a pipe of wine ! —
So may her minstrel, crowned with royal bays,
Alternate praise her pipe, and pipe her praise !
E'en let him chant his smooth, euphonious lays,

A loftier theme my humbler muse essays;
A mightier monarch be it hers to sing,
And claim her laurel from the Money-King!

Great was King Alfred; and if history state
His actions truly, good as well as great.
Great was the Norman; he whose martial hordes
Taught law and order to the Saxon lords,
With gentler thoughts their rugged minds imbued,
And raised the nation whom he first subdued.
Great was King Bess!—I see the critic smile,
As though the muse mistook her proper style;
But to her purpose she will stoutly cling,
The royal maid was "every inch a King!"
Great was Napoleon,—and I would that fate
Might prove his namesake-nephew half as great;
Meanwhile this hint I venture to advance:—
What France admires is good enough for France!
Great princes were they all; but greater far
Than English King, or mighty Russian Czar,
Or Pope of Rome, or haughty Queen of Spain,
Baron of Germany, or Royal Dane,
Or Gallic Emperor, or Persian Khan,

Or any other merely mortal man,
Is the great monarch that my muse would sing,
That mighty potentate, the Money-King !
His Kingdom vast extends o'er every land,
And nations bow before his high command ;
The weakest tremble, and his power obey,
The strongest honor, and confess his sway.
He rules the Rulers ! — e'en the tyrant Czar
Asks his permission ere he goes to war ;
The Turk, submissive to his royal might,
By his consent has gracious leave to fight ;
Whilst e'en Britannia makes her humblest bow
Before her Barings, not her Barons now,
Or on the Rothschild suppliantly calls,
(Her affluent " uncle " with the golden balls,)
Begs of the Jew that he will kindly spare
Enough to put her trident in repair,
And pawns her diamonds, while she humbly craves
Leave of the Money-King once more to " rule the
    waves ! "

He wears no crown upon his royal head,
But many millions in his purse, instead ;

He keeps no halls of state; but holds his court
In dingy rooms where greed and thrift resort;
In iron chests his wondrous wealth he hoards;
Banks are his parlors; brokers are his lords,
Bonds, bills, and mortgages, his favorite books,
Gold is his food, and coiners are his cooks;
Ledgers, his records; stock-reports, his news;
Merchants, his yeomen, and his bondsmen, Jews;
Kings are his subjects, gamblers are his knaves,
Spendthrifts, his fools, and misers are his slaves!
The good, the bad, his golden favor prize,
The high, the low, the simple, and the wise,
The young, the old, the stately, and the gay, —
All bow obedient to his royal sway!

See where, afar, the bright Pacific shore
Gleams in the sun with sands of shining ore,
His last, great empire rises to the view,
And shames the wealth of India and Peru!
Here, throned within his gorgeous "golden gate,"
He wields his sceptre o'er the rising State;
Surveys his conquest with a joyful eye,
Nor for a greater heaves a single sigh!

2

Here, quite beyond the classic poet's dream,
Pactolus runs in every winding stream;
The mountain cliffs the glittering ore enfold,
And every reed that rustles whispers, "gold!"

If to his sceptre some dishonor clings,
Why should we marvel? — 'tis the fate of Kings! —
Their power too oft perverted by abuse,
Their manners cruel, or their morals loose,
The best at times have wandered far astray
From simple Virtue's unseductive way;
And few, of all, at once could make pretence
To royal robes and rustic innocence!

He builds the house where Christian people pray,
And rears a bagnio just across the way;
Pays to the priest his stinted annual fee;
Rewards the lawyer for his venal plea;
Sends an apostle to the heathen's aid;
And cheats the Choctaws, for the good of trade;
Lifts by her heels an Ellsler to renown,
Or, bribing "Jenny," brings an angel down!
  He builds the Theatres, and gambling Halls,

Lloyds and Almacks, St. Peter's and St. Paul's;
Sin's gay retreats, and Fashion's gilded rooms,
Hotels and Factories, Palaces and Tombs;
Bids Commerce spread her wings to every gale;
Bends to the breeze the pirate's bloody sail;
Helps Science seek new worlds among the stars;
Profanes our own with mercenary wars;
The friend of wrong, the equal friend of right,
Oft may we bless, and oft deplore his might,
As buoyant Hope, or darkening fears prevail,
And good or evil turns the moral scale.

All fitting honor I would fain accord,
Whene'er he builds a temple to the Lord;
But much I grieve he often spends his pelf,
As it were raised in honor of himself;
Or, what were worse, and more profanely odd,
A place to worship some Egyptian God!
I wish his favorite architects were graced
With sounder judgment, and a Christian taste.
   Immortal Wren! what fierce, convulsive shocks
Would jar thy bones within their leaden box,
Could'st thou but look across the briny spray,

And see some churches of the present day! —
The lofty dome of consecrated bricks,
Where all the "orders" in disorder mix,
To form a temple whose incongruous frame
Confounds design and puts the Arts to shame!
Where "styles" discordant on the vision jar,
Where Greek and Roman are again at war,
And, as of old, the unrelenting Goth
Comes down at last and overwhelms them both!

Once on a time I heard a parson say,
(Talking of churches in a sprightly way,)
That there was more Religion in the walls
Of towering "Trinity," or grand "St. Paul's,"
Than one could find, upon the strictest search,
In half the saints within the Christian Church!
A layman sitting at the parson's side,
To this new dogma thus at once replied: —
"If, as you say, Religion has her home
In the mere walls that form the sacred dome,
It seems to me the very plainest case,
To climb the steeple were a growth in grace;
And he to whom the pious strength were given

To reach the highest were the nearest Heaven!"
I thought the answer just; and yet 'tis clear
A solemn aspect, grand and yet severe,
Becomes the house of God. 'Tis hard to say
Who from the proper mark are most astray —
They who erect for holy Christian rites,
A gay Pagoda with its tinsel lights,
Or they who offer to the God of Love,
A gorgeous Temple of the pagan Jove!

Immortal Homer and Tassoni sing
What vast results from trivial causes spring;
How naughty Helen by her stolen joy
Brought woe and ruin to unhappy Troy;
How, for a bucket, rash Bologna sold
More blood and tears than twenty such could
    hold! —
Thy power, O Money, shows results as strange
As aught revealed in History's widest range;
Thy smallest coin of shining silver shows
More potent magic than a conjurer knows!
   In olden times — if classic poets say
The simple truth, as poets do to-day —

When Charon's boat conveyed a spirit o'er
The Lethean water to the Hadean shore,
The fare was just a penny — not too great,
The moderate, regular, Stygian statute rate.
Now, for a shilling, he will cross the stream,
(His paddles whirling to the force of steam!)
And bring, obedient to some wizard power,
Back to the Earth more spirits in an hour,
Than Brooklyn's famous ferry could convey,
Or thine, Hoboken, in the longest day!
Time was when men bereaved of vital breath,
Were calm and silent in the realms of Death;
When mortals dead and decently inurned,
Were heard no more; no traveller returned,
Who once had crossed the dark Plutonian strand,
To whisper secrets of the spirit-land —
Save when perchance some sad, unquiet soul
Among the tombs might wander on parole, —
A well-bred ghost, at night's bewitching noon,
Returned to catch some glimpses of the moon,
Wrapt in a mantle of unearthly white,
(The only *'rapping* of an ancient sprite!)
Stalked round in silence till the break of day,

Then from the Earth passed unperceived away!

Now all is changed; the musty maxim fails,

And dead men *do* repeat the queerest tales!

Alas, that here, as in the books, we see

The travellers clash, the doctors disagree;

Alas, that all, the further they explore,

For all their search are but confused the more!

Ye great departed! — men of mighty mark —

Bacon and Newton, Adams, Adam Clarke,

Edwards and Whitefield, Franklin, Robert Hall,

Calhoun, Clay, Channing, Daniel Webster — all

Ye great quit-tenants of this earthly ball, —

If in your new abodes ye cannot rest,

But must return, O, grant us this request: —

Come with a noble and celestial air,

To prove your title to the names ye bear!

Give some clear token of your heavenly birth!

Write as good English as ye wrote on Earth!

Show not to all, in ranting prose and verse,

The spirit's progress is from bad to worse;

And, what were once superfluous to advise,

Don't tell, I beg you, such egregious lies! —

Or if perchance your agents are to blame,

Don't let them trifle with your honest fame;
Let chairs and tables rest, and " rap " instead,
Ay, " knock " your slippery " Mediums " on the head!

What direful woes the hapless man attend,
Who in the means sees life's supremest end;
The wretched miser, — money's sordid slave, —
His only joy to gather and to save.
For this he wakes at morning's early light,
Toils through the day, and ponders in the night;
For this, — to swell his heap of tarnished gold, —
Sweats in the sun, and shivers in the cold,
And suffers more from hunger every day
Than the starved beggar whom he spurns away.
Death comes erewhile to end his worldly strife;
With all his saving he must lose his life!
Perchance the Doctor might protract his breath,
And stay the dreadful messenger of death;
But none is there to comfort or advise;
'Twould cost a dollar! — so the miser dies.

Sad is the sight when Money's power controls
In wedlock's chains the fate of human souls.

From mine to mint, curst is the coin that parts
In helpless grief two loving human hearts;
Or joins in discord, jealousy and hate,
A sordid suitor to a loathing mate!

   I waive the case, the barren case of those
Who have no hearts to cherish or to lose;
Whose wedded state is but a bargain made
In due accordance with the laws of trade;
When the prim parson joins their willing hands,
To marry City lots to Western lands,
Or in connubial ecstasy to mix
Cash and "collateral;" ten-per-cents with six,
And in soft dalliance securely locks
Impassioned dollars with enamored stocks,
Laugh if you will — and who can well refrain? —
But waste no tears, nor pangs of pitying pain;
Hearts such as these may play the queerest pranks,
But never break — except with breaking banks!

   Yet, let me hint, a thousand maxims prove
Plutus may be the truest friend to *Love.*
"Love in a cottage" cosily may dwell,
But much prefers to have it furnished well! —

A parlor ample, and a kitchen snug,
A handsome carpet, an embroidered rug,
A well-stored pantry, and a tidy maid,
A blazing hearth, a cooling window-shade —
Though merely mortal, money-purchased things,
Have wondrous power to clip Love's errant
            wings !
  "Love in a cottage," isn't just the same,
When wind and water strive to quench his flame;
Too oft it breeds the sharpest discontent,
That puzzling question, "how to pay the rent;"
A smoky chimney may alone suffice
To dim the radiance of the fondest eyes;
A northern blast, beyond the slightest doubt,
May fairly blow the torch of *Hymen* out;
And I have heard a worthy Matron hold,
(As one who knew the truth of what she told,)
Love once was drowned, though reckoned water-proof,
By the mere dripping of a leaky roof !

Full many a wise philosopher has tried
Mankind in fitting orders to divide;
And by their forms, their fashions, and their face,

To group, assort, and classify the race.
One would distinguish people by their books;
Another, quaintly, solely by their cooks;
And one who graced the philosophic bench,
Found these three classes — "women, men, and
    French !
The best remains, of all that I have known,
A broad distinction, brilliant, and my own —
Of all mankind, I classify the lot: —
Those who *have Money*, and those who have *not !*

Think'st thou the line a poet's fiction? — then
Go look abroad upon the ways of men!
Go ask the Banker, with his golden seals;
Go ask the borrower, cringing at his heels;
Go ask the maid who, emulous of woe,
Discards the worthier for the wealthier beau;
Go ask the Parson, when a higher prize
Points with the salary where his *duty* lies;
Go ask the Lawyer, who, in legal smoke,
Stands, like a stoker, redolent of " Coke,"
And swings his arms to emphasize a plea
Made doubly ardent by a golden fee;

Go ask the Doctor, who has kindly sped
Old Crœsus, dying on a damask bed,
While his poor neighbor — wonderful to tell —
Was left to Nature, suffered, and got well!
Go ask the belle in high patrician pride,
Who spurns the maiden nurtured at her side,
Her youth's loved playmate at the village-school,
Ere changing fortune taught the rigid rule
Which marks the loftier from the lowlier lot —
Those who have money from those who have not!

Of all the ills that owe their baneful rise
To wealth o'ergrown, the most despotic vice
Is Circean Luxury; prolific dame
Of mental impotence, and moral shame,
And all the cankering evils that debase
The human form, and dwarf the human race.
See yon strange figure, and a moment scan
That slenderest sample of the genus, man!
Mark, as he ambles, those precarious pegs
Which by their motion must be deemed his legs!
He has a head, — one may be sure of that
By just observing that he wears a hat;

That he has arms is logically plain
From his wide coat-sleeves and his pendant cane;
A tongue as well — the inference is fair,
Since, on occasion, he can lisp and swear.
You ask his use? — that's not so very clear,
Unless to spend five thousand pounds a-year
In modish vices which his soul adores,
Drink, dress, and gaming, horses, hounds, and
    scores
Of other follies which I can't rehearse,
Dear to himself and dearer to his purse.
  No product he of Fortune's fickle dice,
The due result of Luxury and Vice,
Three generations have sufficed to bring
That narrow-chested, pale, enervate thing
Down from a *man* — for marvel as you will,
His huge great-grandsire fought on Bunker-Hill!
Bore, without gloves, a musket through the war;
Came back adorned with many a noble scar;
Labored and prospered at a thriving rate,
And, dying, left his heir a snug estate, —
Which grew apace upon *his* busy hands,
Stocks, ships, and factories, tenements and lands,

All here at last — the money and the race —
The latter ending in that foolish face,
The former wandering, far beyond his aim,
Back to the rough plebeians whence it came!

Enough of censure; let my humble lays
Employ one moment in congenial praise.
Let other pens with pious ardor paint
The selfish virtues of the cloistered saint;
In lettered marble let the stranger read
Of him who, dying, did a worthy deed,
And left to charity the cherished store
Which, to his sorrow, he could hoard no more.
I venerate the nobler man who gives
His generous dollars while the donor lives;
Gives with a heart as liberal as the palms
That to the needy spread his honored alms;
Gives with a head whose yet unclouded light
To worthiest objects points the giver's sight;
Gives with a hand still potent to enforce
His well-aimed bounty, and direct its course; —
Such is the giver who must stand confest
In giving glorious, and supremely blest!

One such as this the captious world could find
In noble Perkins, angel of the blind;
One such as this in princely Lawrence shone,
Ere heavenly kindred claimed him for their own!

To me the boon may gracious Heaven assign, —
No cringing suppliant at Mammon's shrine,
Nor slave of Poverty, — with joy to share
The happy mean expressed in Agur's prayer : —
A house (my own) to keep me safe and warm,
A shade in sunshine, and a shield in storm;
A generous board, and fitting raiment, clear
Of debts and duns throughout the circling year;
Silver and gold, in moderate store, that I
May purchase joys that only these can buy;
Some gems of art, a cultured mind to please,
Books, pictures, statues, literary ease.
That " Time is Money " prudent Franklin shows
In rhyming couplets, and sententious prose.
O, had he taught the world, in prose and rhyme,
The higher truth that Money may be Time!
And showed the people, in his pleasant ways,
The art of coining dollars into days!

Days for improvement, days for social life,
Days for your God, your children, and your wife;
Some days for pleasure, and an hour to spend
In genial converse with an honest friend.
Such days be mine!—and grant me, Heaven, but
this,
With blooming health, man's highest earthly bliss,—
And I will read, without a sigh or frown,
The startling news that stocks are going down;
Hear without envy that a stranger hoards
Or spends more treasure than a mint affords;
See my next neighbor pluck a golden plum,
Calm and content within my cottage-home;
Take for myself what honest thrift may bring,
And for his kindness, bless the Money-King!

I'M GROWING OLD.

My days pass pleasantly away;
  My nights are blest with sweetest sleep;
I feel no symptoms of decay;
  I have no cause to mourn nor weep;
My foes are impotent and shy;
  My friends are neither false nor cold,
And yet, of late, I often sigh —
             I'm growing old!

My growing talk of olden times,
  My growing thirst for early news,
My growing apathy to rhymes,
  My growing love of easy shoes,
My growing hate of crowds and noise,
  My growing fear of taking cold,
All whisper in the plainest voice,
             I'm growing old!

3

I'm growing fonder of my staff;
   I'm growing dimmer in the eyes;
I'm growing fainter in my laugh;
   I'm growing deeper in my sighs;
I'm growing careless of my dress;
   I'm growing frugal of my gold;
I'm growing wise; I'm growing — yes —
          I'm growing old!

I see it in my changing taste;
   I see it in my changing hair;
I see it in my growing waist;
   I see it in my growing heir;
A thousand signs proclaim the truth,
   As plain as truth was ever told,
That even in my vaunted youth,
          I'm growing old!

Ah me! — my very laurels breathe
   The tale in my reluctant ears,
And every boon the Hours bequeathe
   But makes me debtor to the Years!

E'en Flattery's honeyed words declare
  The secret she would fain withhold,
And tells me in " How young you are ! "
        I'm growing old !

Thanks for the years ! — whose rapid flight
  My sombre muse too sadly sings ;
Thanks for the gleams of golden light
  That tint the darkness of their wings ;
The light that beams from out the sky,
  Those Heavenly mansions to unfold
Where all are blest, and none may sigh,
       " I'm growing old ! "

SPES EST VATES.

THERE is a saying of the ancient sages:
  No noble human thought,
However buried in the dust of ages,
  Can ever come to nought.

With kindred faith, that knows no base dejection,
  Beyond the sages' scope
I see, afar, the final resurrection
  Of every glorious hope.

I see, as parcel of a new creation,
  The beatific hour
When every bud of lofty aspiration
  Shall blossom into flower.

We are not mocked; it was not in derision
  God made our spirits free;

The poet's dreams are but the dim prevision
  Of blessings that shall be, —

When they who lovingly have hoped and trusted,
  Despite some transient fears,
Shall see Life's jarring elements adjusted,
  And rounded into spheres !

THE WAY OF THE WORLD.

I.

A YOUTH would marry a maiden,
  For fair and fond was she;
But she was rich, and he was poor,
  And so it might not be.

    A lady never could wear, —
      Her mother held it firm, —
    A gown that came of an India plant,
      Instead of an India worm! —

And so the cruel word was spoken;
And so it was two hearts were broken.

II.

A youth would marry a maiden,
  For fair and fond was she;
But he was high and she was low,
  And so it might not be.

A man who had worn a spur,
  In ancient battle won,
Had sent it down with great renown,
  To goad his future son! —
And so the cruel word was spoken;
And so it was two hearts were broken.

III.

A youth would marry a maiden,
  For fair and fond was she;
But their sires disputed about the Mass,
  And so it might not be.
  A couple of wicked Kings,
    Three hundred years agone,
    Had played at a royal game of chess,
      And the church had been a pawn! —
And so the cruel word was spoken;
And so it was two hearts were broken.

THE HEAD AND THE HEART.

The head is stately, calm and wise,
　And bears a princely part;
And down below in secret lies
　The warm, impulsive heart.

The lordly head that sits above,
　The heart that beats below,
Their several office plainly prove,
　Their true relation show.

The head erect, serene and cool,
　Endowed with Reason's art,
Was set aloft to guide and rule
　The throbbing, wayward heart.

And from the head, as from the higher,
　Comes every glorious thought;

And in the heart's transforming fire
All noble deeds are wrought.

Yet each is best when both unite
To make the man complete;
What were the heat without the light?
The light, without the heat?

MY CASTLE IN SPAIN.

THERE's a castle in Spain, very charming to see,
   Though built without money or toil;
Of this handsome estate I am owner in fee,
   And paramount lord of the soil;
And oft as I may I'm accustomed to go
And live, like a king, in my Spanish Chateau!

There's a dame most bewitchingly rounded and
     ripe,
   Whose wishes are never absurd;
Who doesn't object to my smoking a pipe,
   Nor insist on the ultimate word;
In short, she's the pink of perfection, you know;
And she lives, like a queen, in my Spanish Cha-
     teau!

I've a family too; the delightfullest girls,
   And a bevy of beautiful boys;

All quite the reverse of those juvenile churls
 Whose pleasure is mischief and noise;
No modern *Cornelia* might venture to show
Such jewels as those in my Spanish Chateau!

I have servants who seek their contentment in mine,
 And always mind what they are at;
Who never embezzle the sugar and wine,
 And slander the innocent cat;
Neither saucy, nor careless, nor stupidly slow,
Are the servants who wait in my Spanish Cha-
  teau!

I have pleasant companions; most affable folk;
 And each with the heart of a brother;
Keen wits who enjoy an antagonist's joke;
 And beauties who're fond of each other;
Such people, indeed, as you never may know,
Unless you should come to my Spanish Chateau!

I have friends, whose commission for wearing the
  name,
 In kindness unfailing, is shown;

Who pay to another the duty they claim,
    And deem his successes their own;
Who joy in his gladness, and weep at his woe;
You 'll find them (where else?) in my Spanish
        Chateau!

"*O si sic semper!*" I oftentimes say,
    (Though 'tis idle, I know, to complain,)
To think that again I must force me away
    From my beautiful castle in Spain!
Ah! would that my stars had determined it so
I might live the year round in my Spanish Cha-
        teau!

'Tis twenty years, and something more,
  Since, all athirst for useful knowledge,
I took some draughts of classic lore,
  Drawn, very mild, at ———rd College;
Yet I remember all that one
  Could wish to hold in recollection;
The boys, the joys, the noise, the fun;
  But not a single Conic Section.

I recollect those harsh affairs,
  The morning bells that gave us panics,
I recollect the formal prayers,
  That seemed like lessons in Mechanics;
I recollect the drowsy way
  In which the students listened to them,
As clearly, in my wig, to-day,
  As when, a boy, I slumbered through them.

I recollect the tutors all
  As freshly now, if I may say so,
As any chapter I recall
  In Homer or Ovidius Naso.
I recollect, extremely well,
  "Old Hugh," the mildest of fanatics;
I well remember Matthew Bell,
  But very faintly, Mathematics.

I recollect the prizes paid
  For lessons fathomed to the bottom;
(Alas, that pencil-marks should fade!)
  I recollect the chaps who got 'em —
The light equestrians who soared
  O'er every passage reckoned stony;
And took the chalks, — but never scored
  A single honor to the pony!

Ah me! — what changes Time has wrought,
  And how predictions have miscarried! —
A few have reached the goal they sought,
  And some are dead, and some are married;

And some in city journals war;
  And some as politicians bicker;
And some are pleading at the bar;
  For jury-verdicts, or for liquor!

And some on Trade and Commerce wait;
  And some in schools with dunces battle;
And some the gospel propagate;
  And some the choicest breeds of cattle;
And some are living at their ease;
  And some were wrecked in "the revulsion;"
Some serve the State for handsome fees,
  And one, I hear, upon compulsion!

LAMONT, who, in his college days,
  Thought e'en a cross a moral scandal,
Has left his Puritanic ways,
  And worships now with bell and candle;
And MANN, who mourned the negro's fate,
  And held the slave as most unlucky,
Now holds him, at the market rate,
  On a plantation in Kentucky!

Tom Knox, who swore in such a tone
  It fairly might be doubted whether
It really was himself alone,
  Or *Knox* and Erebus together, —
Has grown a very altered man,
  And, changing oaths for mild entreaty,
Now recommends the Christian plan
  To savages in Otaheite!

Alas, for young ambition's vow,
  How envious Fate may overthrow it! —
Poor Harvey is in Congress now,
  Who struggled long to be a poet;
Smith carves (quite well) memorial stones,
  Who tried in vain to make the law go;
Hall deals in hides; and "Pious Jones"
  Is dealing faro in Chicago!

And, sadder still, the brilliant Hays,
  Once honest, manly, and ambitious,
Has taken latterly to ways,
  Extremely profligate and vicious;

By slow degrees — I can't tell how —
  He's reached at last the very groundsel,
And in New York he figures now,
  A member of the Common Council!

4

Madam, — you are very pressing,
  And I can't decline the task ;
With the slightest gift of guessing,
  You would scarcely need to ask !

Don't you see a hint of marriage
  In his sober-sided face ?
In his rather careless carriage,
  And extremely rapid pace ?

If he 's not committed treason,
  . Or some wicked action done,
Can you see the faintest reason
  Why a bachelor should run ?

Why should *he* be in a flurry ?
  But a loving wife to greet,

Is a circumstance to hurry
  The most dignified of feet!

When afar the man has spied her,
  If the grateful, happy elf
Does not haste to be beside her,
  He must be beside himself!

It is but a trifle, may be —
  But observe his practised tone,
When he calms your stormy baby,
  Just as if it were his own!

Do you think a certain meekness
  You have mentioned in his looks,
Is a chronic optic weakness
  That has come of reading books?

Did you ever see his vision
  Peering underneath a hood,
Save enough for recognition,
  As a civil person should!

Could a Capuchin be colder
  When he glances, as he must,
At a finely-rounded shoulder,
  Or a proudly-swelling bust?

Madam! — think of every feature,
  Then deny it, if you can,
He 's a fond, connubial creature,
  And a *very* married man!

" GOD bless the man who first invented sleep ! "
   So Sancho Panza said, and so say I :
And bless him, also, that he didn't keep
   His great discovery to himself; nor try
To make it, — as the lucky fellow might, —
A close monopoly by patent right !

Yes — bless the man who first invented sleep,
   (I really can't avoid the iteration ;)
But blast the man with curses loud and deep,
   Whate 'er the rascal's name, or age, or station,
Who first invented, and went round advising,
That artificial cut-off — Early Rising !

" Rise with the lark, and with the lark to bed,"
   Observes some solemn sentimental owl ;
Maxims like these are very cheaply said ;
   But, ere you make yourself a fool or fowl,

Pray, just inquire about his rise and fall,
And whether larks have any beds at all! '

"The time for honest folks to be a bed"
  Is in the morning, if I reason right;
And he who cannot keep his precious head
  Upon his pillow till it's fairly light,
And so enjoy his forty morning winks,
Is up to knavery; or else — he drinks!

Thomson, who sung about the "Seasons," said
  It was a glorious thing to *rise* in season;
But then he said it — lying — in his bed,
  At ten o'clock A. M., — the very reason
He wrote so charmingly. The simple fact is,
His preaching wasn't sanctioned by his practice.

'Tis, doubtless, well to be sometimes awake, —
  Awake to duty, and awake to truth, —
But when, alas! a nice review we take
  Of our best deeds and days, we find, in sooth,
The hours that leave the slightest cause to weep
Are those we passed in childhood or asleep!

'Tis beautiful to leave the world awhile
    For˙ the soft visions of the gentle night;
And free, at last, from mortal care or guile,
    To live as only in the angels' sight,
In sleep's sweet realm so cosily shut in,
Where, at the worst, we only *dream* of sin!

So, let us sleep, and give the Maker praise.
    I like the lad who, when his father thought
To clip his morning nap by hackneyed phrase
    Of vagrant worm by early songster caught,
Cried, " Served him right! — it's not at all sur-
        prising ;
The worm was punished, sir, for early rising ! "

IDEAL.

Some years ago, when I was young,
  And Mrs. Jones was Miss Delancy;
When wedlock's canopy was hung
  With curtains from the loom of fancy;
I used to paint my future life
  With most poetical precision, —
My special wonder of a wife;
  My happy days; my nights Elysian.

I saw a lady, rather small,
  (A Juno was my strict abhorrence,)
With flaxen hair, contrived to fall
  In careless ringlets, à la Lawrence;
A blonde complexion; eyes that drew
  From autumn clouds their azure brightness;
The foot of Venus; arms whose hue
  Was perfect in its milky whiteness!

I saw a party, quite select, —
   There might have been a baker's dozen ;
A parson, of the ruling sect ;
   A bridemaid, and a city cousin ;
A formal speech to me and mine,
   (Its meaning I could scarce discover ;)
A taste of cake ; a sip of wine ;
   Some kissing — and the scene was over !

I saw a baby — one — no more ;
   A cherub pictured, rather faintly,
Beside a pallid dame who wore
   A countenance extremely saintly.
I saw — but nothing could I hear,
   Except the softest prattle, may be,
The merest breath upon the ear —
   So quiet was that blesséd baby !

REAL.

I see a woman, rather tall,
   And yet, I own, a comely lady ;
Complexion — such as I must call
   (To be exact) a little shady ;

A hand not handsome, yet confest
   A generous one for love or pity ;
A nimble foot, and — neatly dressed
   In No. 5 — extremely pretty !

I see a group of boys and girls
   Assembled round the knee paternal ;
With ruddy cheeks and tangled curls,
   And manners not at all supernal.
And one has reached a manly size ;
   And one aspires to woman's stature ;
And one is quite a recent prize,
   And all abound in human nature !

The boys are hard to keep in trim ;
   The girls are often rather trying ;
And baby — like the cherubim —
   Seems very fond of steady crying !
And yet the precious little one,
   His mother's dear, despotic master,
Is worth a thousand babies done
   In Parian or in alabaster !

And oft that stately dame and I,

    When laughing o'er our early dreaming,

And marking, as the years go by,

    How idle was our youthful scheming, —

Confess the wiser Power that knew

    How *Duty* every joy enhances,

And gave us blessings rich and true,

    And better far than all our fancies!

HOW THE MONEY GOES.

How goes the Money? — Well,
I'm sure it isn't hard to tell;
It goes for rent, and water-rates,
For bread and butter, coal and grates,
Hats, caps, and carpets, hoops and hose, —
And that's the way the Money goes!

How goes the Money? — Nay,
Don't everybody know the way?
It goes for bonnets, coats, and capes,
Silks, satins, muslins, velvets, crapes,
Shawls, ribbons, furs, and furbelows, —
And that's the way the Money goes!

How goes the Money? — Sure,
I wish the ways were something fewer;
It goes for wages, taxes, debts;
It goes for presents, goes for bets,

For paint, *pommade*, and *eau de rose*, —
And that's the way the Money goes!

How goes the Money? — Now,
I 've scarce begun to mention how;
It goes for laces, feathers, rings,
Toys, dolls — and other baby-things,
Whips, whistles, candies, bells, and bows, —
And that's the way the Money goes!

How goes the Money? — Come,
I know it doesn't go for rum;
It goes for schools and Sabbath chimes,
It goes for charity — sometimes;
For missions, and such things as those, —
And that's the way the Money goes!

How goes the Money? — There!
I 'm out of patience, I declare;
It goes for plays, and diamond-pins,
For public alms, and private sins,
For hollow shams, and silly shows, —
And that's the way the Money goes!

TALE OF A DOG.

IN TWO PARTS.

PART FIRST.

I.

"Curse on all curs!" I heard a cynic cry;
  A wider malediction than he thought, —
For what's a cynic? — Had he cast his eye
  Within his dictionary, he had caught
This much of learning, — the untutored elf, —
That he, unwittingly, had cursed himself!

II.

"Beware of dogs," the great Apostle writes;
  A rather brief and sharp philippic sent
To the Philippians. The paragraph invites
  Some little question as to its intent,
Among the best expositors; but then
I find they all agree that "dogs" meant *men!*

III.

Beware of men! a moralist might say,
  And women too; 't were but a prudent hint,
Well worth observing in a general way,
  But having surely no conclusion in 't,
(As saucy satirists are wont to rail,)
All men are faithless, and all women frail.

IV.

And so of dogs 't were wrong to dogmatize
  Without discrimination or degree;
For one may see, with half a pair of eyes,
  That they have characters as well as we:
I hate the rascal who can walk the street
Caning all canines he may chance to meet.

V.

I had a dog that was not all a dog,
  For in his nature there was something human;
Wisely he looked as any pedagogue;
  Loved funerals and weddings, like a woman;
With this (still human) weakness, I confess,
Of always judging people by their dress.

VI.

He hated beggars, it was very clear,
    And oft was seen to drive them from the door;
But that was education; — for a year,
    Ere yet his puppyhood was fairly o'er,
He lived with a Philanthropist, and caught
His practices; the precepts he forgot!

VII.

Which was a pity; yet the dog, I grant,
    Led, on the whole, a very worthy life.
To teach you industry, " Go to the ant, "
    (I mean the insect, not your uncle's wife;)
But — though the counsel sounds a little rude —
Go to the dogs, for love and gratitude.

PART SECOND.

VIII.

" Throw physic to the dogs," the poet cries;
    A downright insult to the canine race;
There's not a puppy but is far too wise
    To put a pill or powder in his face.

Perhaps the poet merely meant to say,
That physic, thrown to dogs, is thrown away —

IX.

Which (as the parson said about the dice)
  Is the best throw that any man can choose;
Take, if you 're ailing, medical advice, —
  Minus the medicine — which, of course, refuse.
Drugging, no doubt, occasioned Homœopathy,
And all the dripping horrors of Hydropathy.

X.

At all events, 'tis fitting to remark,
  Dogs spurn at drugs; their daily bark and whine
Are not at all the musty wine and bark
  The doctors give to patients in decline;
And yet a dog who felt a fracture's smart
Once thanked a kind chirurgeon for his art.

XI.

I 've heard a story, and believe it true,
  About a dog that chanced to break his leg;
His master set it, and the member grew

5

Once more a sound and serviceable peg;
And how d'ye think the happy dog exprest
The grateful feelings of his glowing breast? —

XII.

'Twas not in words; the customary pay
　Of human debtors for a friendly act;
For dogs their thoughts can neither sing nor say,
　E'en in "dog-latin," which (a curious fact)
Is spoken only, — as a classic grace, —
By grave Professors of the human race!

XIII.

No, 'twas in deed; the very briefest tail
　Declared his deep emotions at his cure;
Short, but significant; — one could not fail,
　From the mere wagging of his cynosure
("Surgens e *puppi*"), and his ears agog,
To see the fellow was a grateful dog!

XIV.

One day — still mindful of his late disaster —
　He wandered off the village to explore;

And brought another dog unto his master,
  Lame of a leg, as he had been before;
As who should say—"you see!—the dog is lame,—
You doctored me, pray, doctor him the same!"

xv.

So runs the story, and you have it cheap—
  Dog-cheap, as doubtless such a tale should be;
The moral, surely, isn't hard to reap:—
  Be prompt to listen unto mercy's plea;
The good you get, diffuse; it will not hurt you
E'en from a dog to learn a Christian virtue!

LITTLE JERRY, THE MILLER.

A BALLAD.

BENEATH the hill you may see the mill,
   Of wasting wood and crumbling stone;
The wheel is dripping and clattering still,
   But JERRY, the miller, is dead and gone.

Year after year, early and late,
   Alike in summer and winter weather,
He pecked the stones and calked the gate,
   And mill and miller grew old together.

"Little Jerry!" — 'twas all the same, —
   They loved him well who called him so;
And whether he'd ever another name,
   Nobody ever seemed to know.

'Twas "Little Jerry, come grind my rye;"
   And "Little Jerry, come grind my wheat;"

And " Little Jerry " was still the cry,
   From matron bold and maiden sweet.

'Twas " Little Jerry " on every tongue,
   And so the simple truth was told;
For Jerry was little when he was young,
   And Jerry was little when he was old.

But what in size he chanced to lack,
   That Jerry made up in being strong;
I 've seen a sack upon his back
   As thick as the miller, and quite as long.

Always busy, and always merry,
   Always doing his very best,
A notable wag was Little Jerry,
   Who uttered well his standing jest.

How Jerry lived is known to fame,
   But how he died there 's none may know;
One autumn day the rumor came —
   " The brook and Jerry are very low."

And then 'twas whispered, mournfully,
　The leech had come, and he was dead;
And all the neighbors flocked to see; —
　" Poor Little Jerry ! " was all they said.

They laid him in his earthy bed —
　His miller's coat his only shroud —
" Dust to dust," the parson said,
　And all the people wept aloud.

For he had shunned the deadly sin,
　And not a grain of over-toll
Had ever dropped into his bin,
　To weigh upon his parting soul.

Beneath the hill there stands the mill,
　Of wasting wood and crumbling stone;
The wheel is dripping and clattering still,
　But JERRY, the miller, is dead and gone.

HOW CYRUS LAID THE CABLE.

A BALLAD.

Come, listen all unto my song;
   It is no silly fable;
'Tis all about the mighty cord
   They call the Atlantic Cable.

Bold Cyrus Field he said, says he,
   I have a pretty notion
That I can run a telegraph
   Across' the Atlantic Ocean.

Then all the people laughed, and said,
   They'd like to see him do it;
He might get half-seas-over, but
   He never could go through it;

To carry out his foolish plan
  He never would be able;
He might as well go hang himself
  With his Atlantic Cable!

But Cyrus was a valiant man,
  A fellow of decision;
And heeded not their mocking words,
  Their laughter and derision.

Twice did his bravest efforts fail,
  And yet his mind was stable;
He wa'n't the man to break his heart
  Because he broke his cable.

"Once more, my gallant boys!" he cried;
  " *Three times!* — you know the fable, —
(I'll make it *thirty*," muttered he,
  " But I will lay the cable!")

Once more they tried, — hurrah! hurrah!
  What means this great commotion?

The Lord be praised! the cable 's laid
　Across the Atlantic Ocean!

Loud ring the bells — for, flashing through
　Six hundred leagues of water,
Old Mother England's benison
　Salutes her eldest daughter!

O 'er all the land the tidings speed,
　And soon, in every nation,
They 'll hear about the cable with
　Profoundest admiration!

Now long live James, and long live Vic,
　And long live gallant Cyrus;
And may his courage, faith, and zeal
　With emulation fire us;

And may we honor evermore
　The manly, bold, and stable;
And tell our sons, to make them brave,
　How Cyrus laid the cable!

THE JOLLY MARINER.

A BALLAD.

IT was a jolly mariner
  As ever hove a log;
He wore his trousers wide and free,
  And always ate his prog,
And blessed his eyes, in sailor-wise,
  And never shirked his grog.

Up spoke this jolly mariner,
  Whilst walking up and down : —
" The briny sea has pickled me,
  And done me very brown ;
But here I goes, in these here clo'es,
  A-cruising in the town ! "

The first of all the curious things
  That chanced his eye to meet,

As this undaunted mariner
  Went sailing up the street,
Was, tripping with a little cane,
  A dandy all complete!

He stopped, — that jolly mariner, —
  And eyed the stranger well : —
"What that may be," he said, says he,
  "Is more than I can tell ;
But ne'er before, on sea or shore,
  Was such a heavy swell!"

He met a lady in her hoops,
  And thus she heard him hail : —
"Now blow me tight! — but there's a sight
  To manage in a gale!
I never saw so small a craft
  With such a spread o' sail!

"Observe the craft before and aft, —
  She'd make a pretty prize!"
And then in that improper way
  He spoke about his eyes,

That mariners are wont to use
  In anger or surprise.

He saw a plumber on a roof,
  Who made a mighty din : —
" Shipmate, ahoy ! " the rover cried,
  " It makes a sailor grin
To see you copper-bottoming
  Your upper-decks with tin ! "

He met a yellow-bearded man,
  And asked about the way ;
But not a word could he make out
  Of what the chap would say,
Unless he meant to call him names,
  By screaming, " Nix furstay ! "

Up spoke this jolly mariner,
  And to the man said he,
" I have n't sailed these thirty years
  Upon the stormy sea,
To bear the shame of such a name
  As I have heard from thee !

So take thou that!" — and laid him flat;
　　But soon the man arose,
And beat the jolly mariner
　　Across his jolly nose,
Till he was fain, from very pain,
　　To yield him to the blows.

'Twas then this jolly mariner,
　　A wretched jolly tar,
Wished he was in a jolly-boat
　　Upon the sea afar,
Or riding fast, before the blast,
　　Upon a single spar!

'Twas then this jolly mariner
　　Returned unto his ship,
And told unto the wondering crew
　　The story of his trip,
With many oaths and curses, too,
　　Upon his wicked lip! —

As hoping — so this mariner
　　In fearful words harangued —

His timbers might be shivered, and
  His le 'ward scuppers danged,
(A double curse, and vastly worse
  Than being shot or hanged!)

If ever he — and here again
  A dreadful oath he swore —
If ever he, except at sea,
  Spoke any stranger more,
Or like a son of — something — went
  A-cruising on the shore!

YE TAILYOR-MAN.

A CONTEMPLATIVE BALLAD.

RIGHT jollie is ye tailyor-man,
  As annie man may be;
And all ye daye upon ye benche
  He worketh merrilie.

And oft ye while in pleasante wise
  He coileth up his lymbes,
He singeth songs ye like whereof
  Are not in Watts his hymns.

And yet he toileth all ye while
  His merrie catches rolle;
As true unto ye needle as
  Ye needle to ye pole.

What cares ye valiant tailyor-man
  For all ye cowarde feares?
Against ye scissors of ye Fates
  He pointes his mightie sheares.

He heedeth not ye anciente jests
  That witlesse sinners use;
What feareth ye bolde tailyor-man
  Ye hissinge of a goose?

He pulleth at ye busie threade,
  To feede his lovinge wife
And eke his childe; for unto them
  It is ye threade of life.

He cutteth well ye riche man's coate,
  And with unseemlie pride
He sees ye little waistcoate in
  Ye cabbage bye his side.

Meanwhile ye tailyor-man his wife,
  To labor nothinge loth,

Sits bye with readie hande to baste
  Ye urchin and ye cloth.

Full happie is ye tailyor-man,
  Yet is he often tried,
Lest he, from fullnesse of ye dimes,
  Waxe wanton in his pride.

Full happie is ye tailyor-man,
  And yet he hath a foe,
A cunninge enemie that none
  So well as tailyors knowe.

It is ye slipperie customer
  Who goes his wicked wayes,
And weares ye honest tailyor's coate,
  But never, never payes!

6

TOWN AND COUNTRY.

AN ECLOGUE.

CLOVERTOP.

I've thought, my Cousin, it's extremely queer
That you, who love to spend your August here,
Don't bring, at once, your wife and children down,
And quit, for good, the noisy, dusty town.

SHILLINGSIDE.

Ah! simple swain, this sort of life may do
For such a verdant Clovertop as you,
Content to vegetate in summer air,
And hibernate in winter — like a bear!

CLOVERTOP.

Here we have butter pure as virgin gold,
And milk from cows that can a tail unfold
With bovine pride; and new-laid eggs, whose praise
Is sung by pullets with their morning lays;

Trout from the brook; good water from the well;
And other blessings more than I can tell!

SHILLINGSIDE.

There, simple rustic, we have nightly plays,
And operatic music — charming ways
Of spending time and money — lots of fun;
The Central Park — whene'er they get it done;
Barnum's Museum, full of things erratic,
Terrene, amphibious, airy, and aquatic!

CLOVERTOP.

Here we have rosy, radiant, romping girls,
With lips of rubies, and with teeth of pearls;
I dare not mention half their witching charms;
But, ah! the roundness of their milky arms,
And, oh! what polished shoulders they display,
Bending o'er tubs upon a washing-day!

SHILLINGSIDE.

There we have ladies most superbly made
(By fine *artistes*, who understand their trade),
Who dance the German, flirt a graceful fan,

And speak *such* French as no Parisian can;
Who sing much louder than your country thrushes,
And wear (thank Phalon!) far more brilliant
    blushes!

CLOVERTOP.

Here, boastful Shilling, we have flowery walks,
Where you may stroll, and hold delightful talks,
(No saucy placard frowning as you pass,
" Ten dollars' fine for walking on the grass! ")
Dim-lighted groves, where love's delicious words
Are breathed to music of melodious birds.

SHILLINGSIDE.

There, silly Clover, dashing belles we meet,
Sweeping with silken robes the dusty street;
May gaze into their faces as they pass,
Beneath the rays of dimly-burning gas,
Or, standing at a crossing when it rains,
May see some pretty ankles for our pains.

CLOVERTOP.

Here you may angle for the speckled trout,

Play him awhile, with gentle hand, about,
Then, like a sportsman, pull the fellow out!

SHILLINGSIDE.

There, too, is fishing quite as good, I ween,
Where careless, gaping gudgeons oft are seen,
Rich as yon pasture, and almost as green!

CLOVERTOP.

Here you may see the meadow's grassy plain,
Ripe, luscious fruits, and shocks of golden grain;
And view, luxuriant in a hundred fields,
The gorgeous wealth that bounteous Nature yields!

SHILLINGSIDE.

There you may see Trade's wondrous strength and
        pride,
Where merchant-navies throng on every side,
And view, collected in Columbia's mart,
Alike the wealth of Nature and of Art!

CLOVERTOP.

Cease, clamorous cit! I love these quiet nooks,

Where one may sleep, or dawdle over books,
Or, if he wish of gentle love to dream,
May sit and muse by yonder babbling stream —

SHILLINGSIDE.

Dry up your babbling stream! my Clovertop —
You 're getting garrulous; it 's time to stop.
I love the city, and the city's smoke;
The smell of gas; the dust of coal and coke;
The sound of bells; the tramp of hurrying feet;
The sight of pigs and Paphians in the street;
The jostling crowd; the never-ceasing noise
Of rattling coaches, and vociferous boys;
The cry of "Fire!" and the exciting scene
Of heroes running with their mad "mersheen;"
Nay, now I think that I could even stand
The direful din of Barnum's brazen band,
So much I long to see the town again!
Good-bye! I 'm going by the evening train!
Don't fail to call whene'er you come to town,
We 'll do the city, boy, and do it brown;
I 've really had a pleasant visit here,
And mean to come again another year.

MY FAMILIAR.

Ecce iterum Crispinus!

I.

AGAIN I hear that creaking step! —
  He's rapping at the door! —
Too well I know the boding sound
  That ushers in a bore.
I do not tremble when I meet
  The stoutest of my foes,
But Heaven defend me from the friend
  Who comes — but never goes!

II.

He drops into my easy chair,
  And asks about the news;
He peers into my manuscript,
  And gives his candid views;

He tells´ where he likes the line,
  And where he's forced to grieve;
He takes the strangest liberties, —
  But never takes his leave!

III.

He reads my daily paper through,
  Before I've seen a word;
He scans the lyric (that I wrote)
  And thinks it quite absurd;
He calmly smokes my last cigar,
  And coolly asks for more;
He opens everything he sees, —
  Except the entry door!

IV.

He talks about his fragile health,
  And tells me of the pains
He suffers from a score of ills
  Of which he ne'er complains;
And how he struggled once with death
  To keep the fiend at bay;

On themes like those away he goes —
But never goes away!

V.

He tells me of the carping words
Some shallow critic wrote;
And every precious paragraph
Familiarly can quote;
He thinks the writer did me wrong;
He 'd like to run him through!
He says a thousand pleasant things —
But never says " Adieu!"

VI.

Whene'er he comes — that dreadful man —
Disguise it as I may,
I know that, like an Autumn rain,
He 'll last throughout the day.
In vain I speak of urgent tasks;
In vain I scowl and pout;
A frown is no extinguisher —
It does not put him out!

VII.

I mean to take the knocker off,
  Put crape upon the door,
Or hint to John that I am gone
  To stay a month or more.
I do not tremble when I meet
  The stoutest of my foes,
But Heaven defend me from the friend
  Who never, never goes!

HOW THE LAWYERS GOT A PATRON SAINT.

A LEGEND OF BRETAGNE.

A LAWYER of Brittany, once on a time,
  When business was flagging at home,
Was sent as a legate to Italy's clime,
  To confer with the Father at Rome.

And what was the message the minister brought?
  To the Pope he preferred a complaint
That each other profession a Patron had got,
  While the Lawyers had never a Saint!

"Very true," said his Holiness, — smiling to find
  An attorney so civil and pleasant, —
"But my very last Saint is already assigned,
  And I can't make a new one at present.

To choose from the *Bar* it were fittest, I think;
  Perhaps you've a man in your eye" —

And his Holiness here gave a mischievous wink
  To a Cardinal sitting near by.

But the lawyer replied, in a lawyer-like way,
  "I know what is modest, I hope ;
I didn't come hither, allow me to say,
  To proffer advice to the Pope ! "

"Very well," said his Holiness, "then we will do
  The best that may fairly be done ;
It don't seem exactly the thing, it is true,
  That the Law should be Saint-less alone.

To treat your profession as well as I can,
  And leave you no cause of complaint,
I propose, as the only quite feasible plan,
  To give you a second-hand Saint.

To the neighboring church you will presently go,
  And this is the plan I advise : —
First, say a few *aves* — a hundred or so —
  Then, carefully bandage your eyes ;

Then (saying more *aves*) go groping around,
   And, touching one object alone,
The Saint you are seeking will quickly be found,
   For the first that you touch is your own."

The lawyer did as his Holiness said,
   Without an omission or flaw;
Then, taking the bandages off from his head,
   What do you think he saw?

There was St. Michael (figured in paint)
   Subduing the Father of Evil;
And the lawyer, exclaiming " Be *thou* our Saint!"
   Was touching the form of the Devil!

THE KING AND THE COTTAGER.

A PERSIAN LEGEND.

I.

PRAY list unto a legend
  The ancient poets tell;
'T is of a mighty monarch
  In Persia once did dwell;
A mighty queer old monarch
  Who ruled his kingdom well.

II.

" I must build another palace,"
  Observed this mighty King;
" For this is getting shabby
  Along the southern wing;
And, really, for a monarch,
  It is n't quite the thing.

III.

"So I will have a new one,
    Although I greatly fear,
To build it just to suit me,
    Will cost me rather dear;
And I'd choose, God wot, another spot,
    Much finer than this here."

IV.

So he travelled o'er his kingdom
    A proper site to find,
Where he might build a palace
    Exactly to his mind,
All with a pleasant prospect
    Before it, and behind.

V.

Not long with this endeavor
    The King had travelled round,
Ere, to his royal pleasure,
    A charming spot he found;
But an ancient widow's cabin
    Was standing on the ground.

VI.

" Ah, here," exclaimed the monarch,
　　Is just the proper spot,
If this woman would allow me
　　To remove her little cot."
But the beldam answered plainly,
　　She had rather he would not!

VII.

" Within this lonely cottage,
　　Great Monarch, I was born;
And only from this cottage
　　By Death will I be torn;
So spare it, in your justice,
　　Or spoil it, in your scorn!"

VIII.

Then all the courtiers mocked her,
　　With cruel words and jeers: —
" 'T is plain her royal master
　　She neither loves nor fears;
We would knock her ugly hovel
　　About her ugly ears!

IX.

"When ever was a subject
  Who might the King withstand?
Or deem his spoken pleasure
  As less than his command?
Of course, he'll rout the beldam,
  And confiscate her land!"

X.

But, to their deep amazement,
  His majesty replied: —
"Good woman — never heed them,
  The *King* is on your side;
Your cottage is your castle,
  And here you shall abide.

XI.

To raze it in a moment,
  The power is mine, I grant;
My absolute dominion
  A hundred poets chant;
For being *Khan* of Persia,
  There's nothing that I *can't!*"

7

XII.

('T was in this pleasant fashion
   The mighty monarch spoke;
For Kings have merry fancies
   Like other mortal folk;
And none so high and mighty
   But loves his little joke.)

XIII.

" But power is scarcely worthy
   Of honor or applause,
That in its domination
   Contemns the widow's cause,
Or perpetrates injustice
   By trampling on the laws.

XIV.

" That I have wronged the meanest
   No honest tongue may say;
So bide you in your cottage,
   Good woman, while you may;
What 's yours by deed and purchase
   No man may take away.

XV.

"And I will build beside it, —
    For though your cot may be
In such a lordly presence
    No fitting thing to see,
If it honor not my castle,
    It will surely honor me! —

XVI.

" For so my loyal people
    Who gaze upon the sight,
Shall know that in oppression
    I do not take delight;
Nor hold a King's convenience
    Before a subject's right!"

XVII.

Now from his spoken purpose
    The King departed not;
He built the royal dwelling
    Upon the chosen spot,
And there they stood together,
    The palace and the cot!

XVIII.

Sure such unseemly neighbors
　　Were never seen before;
" His Majesty is doting,"
　　His silly courtiers swore;
But all true loyal subjects,
　　They loved the King the more.

XIX.

Long, long he ruled his kingdom
　　In honor and renown;
But danger ever threatens
　　The head that wears a crown;
And Fortune, tired of smiling,
　　For once put on a frown.

XX.

For ever secret Envy
　　Attends a high estate;
And ever lurking Malice
　　Pursues the good and great;
And ever base Ambition
　　Will end in deadly Hate!

XXI.

And so two wicked courtiers,
  Who long had strove in vain,
By craft and evil counsels,
  To mar the monarch's reign,
Contrived a scheme infernal
  Whereby he should be slain!

XXII.

But as all deeds of darkness
  Are wont to leave a clue
Before the glaring sunlight
  To bring the knaves to view;
That sin may be rewarded,
  And Satan get his due, —

XXIII.

To plan their wicked treason,
  They sought a lonely spot
Behind the royal palace,
  Hard by this widow's cot,
Who heard their machinations,
  And straight revealed the plot!

XXIV.

" I see,"—exclaimed the monarch,
  " The just are wise alone ;
Who spares the rights of others
  May chance to guard his own ;
The widow's humble cottage
  Has propped a monarch's throne ! "

LOVE AND LUCRE.

AN ALLEGORY.

LOVE and LUCRE met one day,
In chill November weather,
And so to while the time away,
They held discourse together.

LOVE at first was rather shy,
As thinking there was danger
In venturing so very nigh
The haughty-looking stranger.

But LUCRE managed to employ
Behavior so potential,
That, in a trice, the bashful boy
Grew bold and confidential.

"I hear," quoth Lucre, bowing low,
  "With all your hearts and honey,
You sometimes suffer — is it so? —
  For lack of mortal money."

Love owned that he was poor in aught
  Except in golden fancies,
And ne'er as yet had given a thought
  To mending his finances;

"Besides, I've heard" — so Love went on,
  The other's hint improving —
"That gold, however sought or won,
  Is not a friend to loving."

"An arrant lie! — as you shall see, —
  Full long ago invented,
By knaves who know not you nor me,
  To tickle the demented."

And Lucre waved his wand, and lo!
  By magical expansion,

Love saw his little hovel grow
    Into a stately mansion!

And where, before, he used to sup
    Untended in his cottage,
And grumble o'er the earthen cup
    That held his meagre pottage, —

Now, smoking viands crown his board,
    And many a flowing chalice;
His larder was with plenty stored,
    And beauty filled the palace!

And Love, though rather lean at first,
    And tinged with melancholy,
On generous wines and puddings nursed,
    Grew very stout and jolly!

Yet, mindful of his early friend,
    He never turns detractor,
But prays that blessings may attend
    His worthy benefactor;

And when his friends are gay above
  Their evening whist or *eucre*,
And drink a brimming health to LOVE,
  He drinks "success to LUCRE!"

DEATH AND CUPID.

AN ALLEGORY.

Ah! — who but oft hath marvelled why
  The gods who rule above
Should e'er permit the young to die,
  The old to fall in love!

Ah! — why should hapless human kind
  Be punished out of season?
Pray listen, and perhaps you'll find
  My rhyme may give the reason.

Death, strolling out one Summer's day,
  Met Cupid, with his sparrows;
And, bantering in a merry way,
  Proposed a change of arrows!

" Agreed ! " — quoth CUPID, — " I foresee
 The queerest game of errors ;
For you the King of Hearts will be !
 And I 'll be King of Terrors ! "

And so 't was done — alas the day
 That multiplied their arts ! —
Each from the other bore away
 A portion of his darts ! —

And that explains the reason why,
 Despite the gods above,
The young are often doomed to die ;
 The old to fall in love !

THE FAMILY MAN.

I was once a jolly young beau,
  And knew how to pick up a fan,
But I've done with all that, you must know,
  For now I'm a family man!

When a partner I ventured to take,
  The ladies all favored the plan;
They vowed I was certain to make
  "Such an excellent family man!"

If I travel by land or by water,
  I have charge of some Susan or Ann;
Mrs. Brown is so sure that her daughter
  Is safe with a family man!

The trunks and the bandboxes round 'em
  With something like horror I scan,
But though I may mutter, "Confound 'em!"
  I smile — like a family man!

I once was as gay as a templar,
  But levity's now under ban;
Young people must have an exemplar,
  And I am a family man!

The club-men I meet in the city
  All treat me as well as they can;
And only exclaim, "What a pity
  Poor Tom is a family man!"

I own I am getting quite pensive;
  Ten children, from David to Dan,
Is a family rather extensive;
  But then — I'm a family man!

NE CREDE COLORI:

OR, TRUST NOT TO APPEARANCES.

THE musty old maxim is wise,
　　Although with antiquity hoary;
What an excellent homily lies
　　In the motto, "*Ne crede colori!*"

A blustering minion of Mars
　　Is vaunting his battles so gory;
You see some equivocal scars,
　　And mutter, *Ne crede colori!*

A fellow solicits your tin
　　By telling a runaway story;
You look at his ebony skin,
　　And think of, *Ne crede colori!*

You gaze upon beauty that vies
  With the rose and the lily in glory;
But certain "inscrutable dyes"
  Remind you, *Ne crede colori!*

There's possibly health in the flush
  That rivals the red of Aurora;
But brandy-and-water can blush,
  And whisper, *Ne crede colori!*

My story is presently done,
  Like the ballad of good Mother Morey;
But all imposition to shun,
  Remember, *Ne crede colori!*

CLARA TO CLOE.

AN EPISTLE FROM A CITY LADY TO A COUNTRY
COUSIN.

DEAR CLOE:—I'm deeply your debtor,
  (Though the mail was uncommonly slow,)
For the very agreeable letter
  You wrote me a fortnight ago.
I know you are eagerly waiting
  For all that I promised to write,
But my pen is unequal to stating
  One half that my heart would indite.

The weather is terribly torrid;
  And writing's a serious task;
The new style of bonnet is horrid;
  And so is the new-fashioned *basque;*
The former — but language would fail
  Were its epithets doubly as strong —
The latter is worn with a tail
  Very ugly and tediously long!

8

And then as to *crinoline* — Gracious !
  If you only could see cousin Ruth —
The pictures, for once, are veracious,
  And editors utter the truth !
I know you will think it a pity;
  And every one makes such a sneer of it ;
But there is n't a saint in the city
  Whose skirts are entirely clear of it !

And then what a fortune of stuff
  To cover the skeleton over ! —
Charles says the idea is enough
  To frighten a sensible lover ;
And, pretending that *we* are to blame
  For every financial declension,
Swears husbands must soon do the same,
  If wives have another " extension ! "

The town is exceedingly dull,
  And so is the latest new farce ;
The parks are uncommonly full,
  But beaux are deplorably scarce ;

They're gone to the " Springs " and the " Falls,"
  To exhibit their greyhounds and graces,
And recruit at, — what Frederick calls —
  The Brandy-and-Watering Places !

Since my former epistle, which carried
  The news of that curious plot ;
Of Miss S. who ran off — and was married ;
  Of Miss B. who ran off — and was not, —
There isn't a whisper of scandal
  To keep gentle ladies in humor,
And Gossip, the pleasant old vandal,
  Is dying for want of a rumor !   CLARA.

P. S. — But wasn't it funny ? —
  Mrs. Jones, at a party last week,
(The lady so proud of her money,
  Of whom you have oft heard me speak,)
Appeared so delightfully stupid,
  When she spoke, through the squeak of her
      phthisic,
Of the statue of Psyche and Cupid
  As " the *statute of Cuppid and Physic !* "   C.

CLOE TO CLARA.

A SARATOGA LETTER.

DEAR CLARA : — I wish you were here :
　　The prettiest spot upon earth !
With everything charming, my dear, —
　　Beaux, badinage, music, and mirth !
Such rows of magnificent trees,
　　Overhanging such beautiful walks,
Where lovers may stroll, if they please,
　　And indulge in the sweetest of talks !

We go every morning, like geese,
　　To drink at the favorite Spring ;
Six tumblers of water a-piece,
　　Is simply the regular thing ;
For such is its wonderful virtue,
　　Though rather unpleasant at first,
No quantity ever can hurt you,
　　Unless you should happen to burst !

And then, what a gossiping sight!
  What talk about William and Harry;
How Julia was spending last night;
  And *why* Miss Morton should marry!
Dear Clara, I 've happened to see
  Full many a tea-table slaughter;
But, really, scandal with tea
  Is nothing to scandal with water!

Apropos of the Spring — have you heard
  The quiz of a gentleman here
On a pompous M. C. who averred
  That the *name* was remarkably queer?
" The Spring, — to keep it from failing, —
  With wood is encompassed about,
And derives, from its permanent *railing*,
  The title of ' Congress,' no doubt ! "

'T is pleasant to guess at the reason —
  The genuine motive which brings
Such all-sorts of folks, in the season,
  To stop a few days at the Springs.

Some come to partake of the waters,
(The sensible, old-fashioned elves,)
Some come to dispose of their daughters,
And some to dispose of — themselves!

Some come to exhibit their faces
To new and admiring beholders ;
Some come to exhibit their graces,
And some to exhibit their shoulders ;
Some come to make péople stare
At the elegant dresses they've got ;
Some to show what a lady may wear,
And some, — what a lady should not!

Some come to squander their treasure,
And some their funds to improve ;
And some for mere love of pleasure,
And some for the pleasure of love ;
And some to escape from the old,
And some to see what is new ;
But most — it is plain to be told —
Come here — because other folks do !

And that, I suppose, is the reason
 Why *I* am enjoying, to-day,
What's called "the height — of the season"
 In rather the loftiest way.
Good-bye — for now I must stop —
 To Charley's command I resign, —
So I'm his for the regular hop,
 But ever most tenderly thine,   Cloe.

WISHING.

Of all amusements for the mind,
  From logic down to fishing,
There is n't one that you can find
  So very cheap as " wishing."
A very choice diversion too,
  If we but rightly use it,
And not, as we are apt to do,
  Pervert it, and abuse it.

I wish — a common wish indeed, —
  My purse were somewhat fatter,
That I might cheer the child of need,
  And not my pride to flatter;
That I might make Oppression reel,
  As only gold can make it,
And break the Tyrant's rod of steel,
  As only gold can break it.

I wish — that Sympathy and Love,
　And every human passion,
That has its origin above,
　Would come and keep in fashion;
That Scorn, and Jealousy, and Hate,
　And every base emotion,
Were buried fifty fathom deep
　Beneath the waves of Ocean!

I wish — that friends were always true,
　And motives always pure;
I wish the good were not so few,
　I wish the bad were fewer;
I wish that parsons ne'er forgot
　To heed their pious teaching;
I wish that practising was not
　So different from preaching!

I wish — that modest worth might be
　Appraised with truth and candor;
I wish that innocence were free
　From treachery and slander;

I wish that men their vows would mind;
  That women ne'er were rovers;
I wish that wives were always kind,
  And husbands always lovers!

I wish — in fine — that Joy and Mirth,
  And every good Ideal,
May come erewhile, throughout the earth,
  To be the glorious Real;
Till God shall every creature bless
  With his supremest blessing,
And Hope be lost in Happiness,
  And Wishing in Possessing!

RICHARD OF GLOSTER.

A TRAVESTIE.

PERHAPS, my dear boy, you may never have heard
Of that wicked old monarch, KING RICHARD THE
  THIRD, —
Whose actions were often extremely absurd;
   And who led such a sad life,
   Such a wanton and mad life;
Indeed, I may say, such a wretchedly bad life,
I suppose I am perfectly safe in declaring,
There was ne'er such a monster of infamous daring;
In all sorts of crime he was wholly unsparing;
In pride and ambition was quite beyond bearing;
And had a bad habit of cursing and swearing.

I must own, my dear boy, I have more than sus-
  pected
The King's education was rather neglected;

And that at *your* school with any two " Dicks "
Whom your excellent teacher diurnally pricks
In his neat little tables, in order to fix
Each pupil's progression with numeral nicks,
Master RICHARD Y. GLOSTER would often have
      heard
His standing recorded as, " Richard — *the third !* "

But whatever of learning his Majesty had,
'T is clear the King's English was shockingly bad,
     At the slightest pretence
     Of disloyal offence,
His anger exceeded all reason or sense ;
And, having no need to foster or nurse it, he
Would open his wrath, then, as if to disperse it, he
Would scatter his curses like College degrees ;
     And, quite at his ease,
     Conferred his " *d-d's.* "
As plenty and cheap as a young University !

And yet Richard's tongue was remarkably smooth ;
Could utter a lie quite as easy as truth ;
(Another bad habit he got in his youth ;)

And had, on occasion, a powerful battery
Of plausible phrases and eloquent flattery,
Which gave him, my boy, in that barbarous day,
(Things are different now, I am happy to say,)
Over feminine hearts a most perilous sway.
The women, in spite of an odious hump
Which he wore on his back, all thought him a
      trump ;
And just when he 'd played them the scurviest trick,
They 'd swear in their hearts that this crooked old
      stick, —
This treacherous, dangerous, dissolute Dick,
For honor and virtue beat Cato all hollow ;
And in figure and face was another Apollo !

      He murdered their brothers,
        And fathers and mothers ;
And, worse than all that, he slaughtered by dozens
His own royal·uncles and nephews and cousins ;
And then, in the cunningest sort of orations,
      In smooth conversations,
      And flattering ovations,
Made love to their principal female relations !

'T was very improper, my boy, you must know,
For the son of a King to behave himself so;
And you 'll scarcely believe what the chronicles
    show
        Of his wonderful wooings,
        And infamous doings;
But here's an exploit that he certainly *did* do —
        Killed his own cousin NED,
        As he slept in his bed,
And married, next day, the disconsolate widow!

I don't understand how such ogres arise,
But beginning, perhaps, with things little in size,
Such as torturing beetles and bluebottle-flies,
Or scattering snuff in a poodle-dog's eyes, —
King Richard had grown so wantonly cruel,
He minded a murder no more than a duel;
He 'd indulge, on the slightest pretence or occasion,
In his favorite amusement of Decapitation,
        Until "Off with his head!"
        It is credibly said,
From his Majesty's mouth came as easy and pat
As from an old constable, "Off with his hat!"

One really shivers,

And fairly quivers,

To think of the treatment of Grey, and Rivers,

And Hastings, and Vaughn, and other good livers,

All suddenly sent, at the tap of a drum,

From the Kingdom of England to Kingdom-Come!

Of Buckingham doomed to a tragical end

For being the tyrant's particular friend;

Of Clarence who died, it is mournful to think,

Of wine that he was n't permitted to drink!

And the beautiful babies of royal blood,

Two little White Roses both nipt in the bud!

And silly Queen Anne — what sorrow it cost her

(And served her right!) for daring to foster

The impudent suit of this Richard of Gloster;

Who, instead of conferring a royal gratuity,

A dower, or even a decent *Anne*-uity,

Just gave her a portion of — something or other

That made her as quiet as Pharaoh's mother!

Ah, Richard! — you 're going it quite too fast;

Your doom is slow, but it 's coming at last;

Your bloody crown
Will topple down,
And you 'll be done uncommonly brown!
Your foes are thick,
My daring Dick,
And RICHMOND, a prince and a regular brick,
Is after you now with a very sharp stick!

On Bosworth field the armies to-night
Are pitching their tents in each other's sight;
And   to-morrow! — to-morrow! — they 're going   to
fight!

And now King Richard has gone to bed;
But e'en in his sleep
He cannot keep
The past or the future out of his head.
In his deep remorse,
Each mangled corse
Of all he had slain, — or, what was worse,
Their ghosts, — came up in terrible force,
And greeted his ear with unpleasant discourse,

Until, with a scream,

He woke from his dream,

And shouted aloud for "another horse!"

Perhaps you may think, my little dear,

King Richard's request was rather queer;

But I'll presently make it exceedingly clear:—

THE ROYAL SLEEPER WAS OVERFED.

I mean to say that, against his habit,

He'd eaten Welch-rabbit

With very bad whiskey on going to bed.

I've had the Night-Mare with horrible force,

And much prefer a different horse!

But see! the murky Night is gone!

The Morn is up, and the Fight is on!

The Knights are engaging, the warfare is waging,

On the right — on the left, the battle is raging;

King Richard is down!

Will he save his crown?

There's a crack in it now!—he's beginning to

bleed!

Aha! King Richard has lost his steed!

9

(At a moment like this 't is a terrible need!)

He shouts aloud with thundering force,

And offers a *very* high price for a horse.

But it's all in vain — the battle is done —

The day is lost! — and the day is won! —

And RICHMOND is King! and RICHARD's a corse!

MORAL.

Remember, my boy, that moral enormities

Are apt to attend corporeal deformities.

Whatever you have, or whatever you lack,

Beware of getting a crook in your back;

And, while you're about it, I'd very much rather

You'd grow tall and superb, *i. e.* copy your father!

Don't learn to be cruel, pray let me advise,

By torturing beetles and bluebottle-flies,

Or scattering snuff in a poodle-dog's eyes.

If you ever should marry, remember to wed

A handsome, plump, modest, sweet-spoken, well-bred,

And sensible maiden of twenty — instead

Of a widow whose husband is recently dead!

If you'd shun in your naps those horrible *Incubi*,
Beware what you eat, and be careful what drink
  you buy;
Or else you. may see, in your sleep's perturbations,
Some old and uncommonly ugly relations,
Who'll be very apt to disturb your nutations
By unpleasant allusions, and rude observations!

HO-HO OF THE GOLDEN BELT.

ONE OF THE "NINE STORIES OF CHINA,"

VERSIFIED AND DIVERSIFIED.

A BEAUTIFUL maiden was little MIN-NE,
Eldest daughter of wise WANG-KE;
Her skin had the color of saffron tea,
And her nose was flat as flat could be;
And never were seen such beautiful eyes,
Two almond-kernels in shape and size,
Set in a couple of slanting gashes,
And not in the least disfigured by lashes;
  And then such feet!
  You'd scarcely meet
In the longest walk through the grandest street,
  (And you might go seeking
  From Nanking to Peeking,)
A pair so remarkably small and neat!
  Two little stumps,
  Mere pedal lumps,

That toddle along with the funniest thumps,

In China, you know, are reckoned trumps.

You guess the owner, the moment you hear 'em,

By the classical rule, " *ex pede Venerem!* "

It seems a trifle, to make such a boast of it;

But how they *will* dress it,

And bandage and press it,

By making the least, to make the most of it!

As you may suppose,

She had plenty of beaux

Bowing around her beautiful toes,

Praising her feet, and eyes, and nose,

In rapturous verse and elegant prose!

She had lots of lovers, old and young;

There was lofty LONG, and babbling LUNG,

Opulent TIN, and eloquent TUNG,

Musical SING, and, the rest among,

Great HANG-YU and YU-BE-HUNG.

But though they smiled and smirked and bowed,

None could please her of all the crowd;

LUNG and TUNG she thought too loud;

Opulent TIN was much too proud;

Lofty LONG was quite too tall;

Musical SING sung very small;

And, most remarkable freak of all,

Of great HANG-YU the lady made game,

And YU-BE-HUNG she mocked the same,

By echoing back his ugly name!

But the hardest heart is doomed to melt;

Love is a passion that *will* be felt;

And just when scandal was making free

To hint "what a pretty old maid she'd be" —

    Little MIN-NE,

    (Who but she?)

Married Ho-Ho of the Golden Belt!

A man, I must own, of bad reputation,

And low in purse, though high in station —

A sort of Imperial poor-relation;

Who ranked as the Emperor's second cousin,

Multiplied by a hundred dozen;

And, to mark the love the Emperor felt,

    Had a pension clear

    Of three pounds a-year,

And the honor of wearing a Golden Belt!

And gallant Ho-Ho
Could really show
A handsome face, as faces go
In the Flowery Land where, you must know,
The finest flowers of beauty grow.
He 'd the very widest kind of jaws,
And his nails were like an eagle's claws,
And — though it may seem a wondrous tail —
(Truth is mighty and will prevail!)
He 'd a *queue* as long as the deepest cause
Under the Emperor's chancery laws!

Yet how he managed to win MIN-NE,
The men declared they could n't see;
But all the ladies, over their tea,
In this one point were known to agree: —
Four gifts were sent to aid his plea:
A smoking-pipe with a golden clog,
A box of tea, and a poodle dog,
And a painted heart that was all a-flame,
And bore, in blood, the lover's name.

Ah! how could presents pretty as these

A delicate lady fail to please?
She smoked the pipe with the golden clog,
And drank the tea, and ate the dog,
And kept the heart, — and that's the way
The match was made, the gossips say.

I can't describe the wedding day,
Which fell in the lovely month of May;
Nor stop to tell of the Honey-Moon,
And how it vanished all too soon;
Alas! that I the truth must speak,
And say, that in the fourteenth week,
Soon as the wedding-guests were gone,
    And their wedding-suits began to doff,
Min-Ne was weeping and "taking on,"
    For *he* had been trying to "take her off!"
Six wives before he had sent to Heaven,
And being partial to number "Seven,"
He wished to add his latest pet,
Just, perhaps, to make up the set.
Mayhap the rascal found a cause
Of discontent in a certain clause
In the Emperor's very liberal laws,

Which gives, when a Golden Belt is wed,
Six hundred pounds to furnish the bed;
And if, in turn, he marry a score,
With every wife six hundred more.

First he tried to murder Min-Ne
With a special cup of poisoned tea;
But the lady, smelling a mortal foe,
　　　Cried " Ho-Ho ! —
I'm very fond of mild Souchong,
But you — my love — you make it too strong!"

At last Ho-Ho, the treacherous man,
Contrived the most infernal plan
Invented since the world began:
He went and got him a savage dog,
Who'd eat a woman as soon as a frog,
Kept him a day without any prog,
Then shut him up in an iron bin,
Slipped the bolt, and locked him in;
　　　Then giving the key
　　　To poor Min-Ne,

Said, " Love, there 's something you *must n't* see
In the chest beneath the orange-tree."

 *   *   *   *   *   *

Poor, mangled MIN-NE ! with her latest breath,
She told her father the cause of her death;
And so it reached the Emperor's ear,
And his Highness said, " It is very clear,
Ho-Ho has committed a murder here ! "

And he doomed Ho-Ho to end his life
By the terrible dog that killed his wife;
But in mercy (let his praise be sung !)
His thirteen brothers were merely hung,
And his slaves bambooed, in the mildest way,
For a calendar month, three times a day;
And that 's the way that JUSTICE dealt
With wicked Ho-Ho of the Golden Belt !

TOM BROWN'S DAY IN GOTHAM.

Qui mores hominum multorum vidit et URBEM.

I 'LL tell you a story of THOMAS BROWN —
I don't mean the poet of Shropshire town ;
Nor the Scotch Professor of wide renown ;
But "Honest Tom Brown ;" so called, no doubt,
  Because with the same
  Identical name,
A good many fellows were roving about
Of whom the sheriff might prudently swear '
That "honest" with them, was a *non-est* affair !

Now Tom was a Yankee of wealth and worth,
Who lived and throve by tilling the Earth ;
  For Tom had wrought
  As a farmer ought,
Who, doomed to toil by original sinning,
Began — like Adam — at the beginning.

He ploughed, he harrowed, and he sowed;
He drilled, he planted, and he hoed;
He dug and delved, and reaped and mowed.
(I wish I could — but I can't — tell now
Whether he used a subsoil-plough;
Or whether, in sooth, he had ever seen
A regular reaping and raking-machine.)

He took most pains
With the nobler grains
Of higher value, and finer tissues
Which, possibly, one
Inclined to a pun,
Would call — like *Harper* — his " *cereal* issues! "
With wheat his lands were all a-blaze;
'T was amazing to look at his fields of maize;
And there were places
That showed *rye*-faces
As pleasant to see as so many Graces.
And as for Hops,
His annual crops,
(So very extensive that, on my soul,
They fairly reached from pole to pole!)

Would beat the guess of any old fogie,

Or — the longest season at Saratoga!

Whatever seed did most abound,

In the grand result that Autumn found,

It was his plan,

Though a moderate man,

To be early running it into the ground;

That is to say,

In another way : —

Whether the seed was barley or hay,

Large or little, or green or gray, —

Provided only it promised to " pay," —

He never chose to labor in vain

By stupidly going against the grain,

But hastened away, without stay or stop,

And carefully put it into his crop.

And he raised tomatoes

And lots of potatoes,

More sorts, in sooth, than I could tell;

Turnips, that always turned up well;

Celery, all that he could sell;

Grapes by the bushel, sour and sweet;

Beets, that certainly could n't be beat;

Cabbage — like some sartorial mound;

Vines, that fairly *cu*-cumbered the ground;

Some pumpkins — more than he could house, and

Ten thousand pears; (that's twenty thousand!)

Fruit of all kinds and propagations,

Baldwins, Pippins, and Carnations,

And apples of other appellations.

To sum it all up in the briefest space,

As you may suppose, Brown flourished apace,

Just because he proceeded, I venture to say,

In the *nulla-retrorsum-vestigi*-ous way;

That is — if you're not University-bred —

He took Crocket's advice about going ahead.

At all the State Fairs he held a fair station,

Raised horses and cows and his own reputation;

Made butter and money; took a Justice's niche;

Grew wheat, wool, and hemp; corn, cattle, and — rich!

But who would be always a country-clown?

　　　And so Tom Brown

　　　Sat himself down,

And, knitting his brow in a studious frown,

　　　He said, says he: —

　　　It's plain to see,

And I think Mrs. B. will be apt to agree,
(If she don't, it's much the same to me,)
   That I, TOM BROWN,
   Should go to town!
But then, says he, what town shall it be?
Boston-town is consid'rably nearer,
And York is farther, and so will be dearer,
But then, of course, the sights will be queerer;
Besides, I'm told, you're surely a lost 'un,
If you once get astray in the streets of Boston.
   York is right-angled;
   And Boston, right-tangled;
And both, I've no doubt, are uncommon new-
  fangled.
Ah!—the "SMITHS," I remember, belong to York,
('Twas ten years ago I sold them my pork,)
Good, honest traders—I'd like to know them—
And so—'t is settled—I'll go to Gotham!

   And so Tom Brown
   Sat himself down,
With many a smile and never a frown,
And rode, by rail, to that notable town

Which I really think well worthy of mention
As being America's greatest invention!
Indeed, I'll be bound that if Nature and Art,
(Though the former, being older, has gotten the
    start,)
In some new Crystal Palace of suitable size,
Should show their *chefs-d'œuvre*, and contend for
    the prize,
The latter would prove, when it came to the
    scratch,
Whate'er you may think, no contemptible match;
For should old Mrs. Nature endeavor to stagger
    her
By presenting, at last, her majestic Niagara;
Miss Art would produce an equivalent work
In her great, overwhelming, unfinished NEW YORK!

      And now Mr. Brown
      Was fairly in town,
In that part of the city they used to call "down,"
Not far from the spot of ancient renown
      As being the scene
      Of the Bowling Green,

A fountain that looked like a huge tureen
Piled up with rocks, and a squirt between;
But the " Bowling " now has gone where they tally
" The Fall of the Ten," in a neighboring alley;
And as to the " Green " — why, that you will find
Whenever you see the " invisible " kind ! —
And he stopped at an Inn that 's known very well,
" Delmonico's " once — now " Stevens's Hotel " ;
(And, to venture a pun which I think rather witty,
There 's no better Inn in this Inn-famous city !)

  And Mr. Brown
   Strolled up town,   .
And I 'm going to write his travels down;
But if you suppose *Tom Brown* will disclose
The usual sins and follies of those
Who leave rural regions to see city-shows —
   You could n't well make
   A greater mistake;
For Brown was a man of excellent sense;
Could see very well through a hole in a fence,
And was honest and plain, without sham or pre-
  tence;

Of sharp, city-learning he could n't have boasted,
But he was n't the chap to be easily roasted;
Though, like many a " Bill," he was n't well
    " posted."
          And here let me say,
In a very dogmatic, oracular way,
(And I 'll prove it, before I have done with my
    lay,)
Not only that honesty 's likely to " pay,"
But that one must be, as a general rule,
At least half a knave to be wholly a fool!

Of pocketbook-dropping, Tom never had heard,
(Or at least if he had, he 'd forgotten the word,)
And now when, at length, the occasion occurred,
For *that* sort of chaff he was n't the bird.
The gentleman argued with eloquent force,
And begged him to pocket the money, of course ;
But Brown, without thinking at all what he said,
Popped out the first thing that entered his head,
(Which chanced to be wondrously fitting and true,)
" No — no — my dear Sir — I 'll be *burnt* if I
    do ! "

Two lively young fellows, of elegant mien,
Amused him awhile with a pretty machine —
An ivory ball, which he never had seen.
But though the unsuspecting stranger
In the "patent safe" saw, no patent danger,
He easily dodged the nefarious net,
Because "he was n't accustomed to bet."

      Ah ! — here, I wot,
        Is exactly the spot
To make a small fortune as easy as not !
That man with the watch — what lungs he has
      got !
It's " Going — the best of that elegant lot —
To close a concern, at a desperate rate, —
The jeweller ruined as certain as fate ! —
A capital watch ! — you may see by the weight —
Worth one hundred dollars as easy as eight —
Or half of that sum to melt down into plate —
(Brown does n't know ' Peter ' from Peter the
      Great)
        But then I can't dwell,
        I 'm ordered to sell,

And mus'n't stand weeping — just look at the
    shell —

I warrant the ticker to operate well —

Nine dollars! — it's hard to be selling it under

A couple of fifties — it's cruel, by Thunder!

Ten dollars! — I'm offered — the man who secures

This splendid — ten dollars! — say twelve, and it's
    yours!"

"Don't want it" — quoth Brown — "I don't wish
    to buy;

Fifty dollars, I'm sure, one could n't call high —

But to see the man *ruined!* — Dear Sir, I de-
    clare —

Between two or three bidders, it does n't seem
    fair;

To knock it off now were surely a sin;

Just wait, my dear Sir, till the people come in! —

Allow me to say, you disgrace your position

As Sheriff — consid'ring the debtor's condition —

To sell *such* a watch without more competition!"

         And here Mr. Brown

         Gave a very black frown,

Stepped leisurely out, and walked farther up town.

To see him stray along Broadway
In the afternoon of a summer's day,
And note what he chanced to see and say;
    And what people he meets
    In the narrower streets,
Were a pregnant theme for a longer lay.
How he marvelled at those geological chaps
Who go poking about in crannies and gaps,
Those curious people in tattered breeches,
The rag-wearing, rag-picking sons of — ditches,
Who find in the very nastiest niches
A "decent living," and sometimes riches;
How he thought city prices exceedingly queer,
The 'busses too cheap, and the hacks too dear;
How he stuck in the mud, and got lost in the
    question —
A problem too hard for his mental digestion —
Why — in cleaning the city, the city employs
Such a very small *corps* of such very small boys;
How he judges by dress, and accordingly makes,
By mixing up classes, the drollest mistakes.
How — as if simple vanity ever were vicious,
Or women of merit could be meretricious, —

He imagines the dashing Fifth-Avenue dames
The same as the girls with unspeakable names!
An exceedingly natural blunder in sooth,
But, I'm happy to say, very far from the truth;
For e'en at the worst, whate'er you suppose,
The one sort of ladies can *choose* their beaux,
While, as to the other — but every one knows
What — if 't were a secret — I would n't disclose.

       And Mr. Brown
       Returned from town,
With a bran new hat, and a muslin gown,
And he told the tale, when the sun was down,
How he spent his eagles, and saved his crown;
How he showed his pluck by resisting the claim
Of an impudent fellow who asked his name;
But paid — as a gentleman ever is willing —
At the old Park-Gate, the regular shilling!

POST-PRANDIAL VERSES.

RECITED AT THE FESTIVAL OF THE PSI UPSILON FRATERNITY, IN BOSTON, JULY 21, 1853.

DEAR Brothers, who sit at this bountiful board,
With excellent viands so lavishly stored,
That, in newspaper phrase, 't would undoubtedly
   groan,
If groaning were but a convivial tone,
Which it is n't — and therefore, by sympathy led,
The table, no doubt, is rejoicing instead.
Dear Brothers, I rise, — and it won't be surprising
If you find me, like bread, all the better for
   rising, —
I rise to express my exceeding delight
In our cordial reunion this glorious night!

Success to "PSI UPSILON!" — Beautiful name! —
To the eye and the ear it is pleasant the same;

Many thanks to old Cadmus who made us his
  debtors,
By inventing, one day, those capital letters
Which still, from the ˙ heart, we shall know how to
  speak
When we've fairly forgotten the rest of our Greek!

To be open and honest in all that you do;
To every high trust to be faithful and true;
In aught that concerns morality's scheme,
To be more ambitious *to be* than to *seem;*
To cultivate honor as higher in worth
Than favor of fortune, or genius, or birth;
By every endeavor to render your lives
As spotless and fair as your — possible wives;
To treat with respect all the innocent rules
That keep us at peace with society's fools;
But to face every *canon* that e'er was designed
To batter a town or beleaguer a mind,
Ere you yield to the Moloch that Fashion has reared
One jot of your freedom, or hair of your beard, —
All this, and much more, I might venture to teach,
Had I only a "call" — and a " license to preach " —

But since I have not, to my modesty true,
I 'll lay it all by — as a layman should do —
And drop a few lines, tipt with Momus's flies,
To angle for shiners — that lurk in your eyes!

May you ne'er get in love or in debt, with a doubt
As to whether or no you will ever get out;
May you ne'er have a mistress who plays the
          coquette,
Or a neighbor who blows on a cracked clarionet;
May you learn the first use of a lock on your door,
And ne'er, like Adonis, be killed by a bore;
Shun canting and canters with resolute force,
(A "canter" is shocking, except in a horse;)
At jovial parties mind what you are at,
Beware of your head and take care of your hat,
Lest you find that a favorite son of your mother
Has a brick in the one and an ache in the other;
May you never, I pray, to worry your life,
Have a weak-minded friend, or a strong-minded wife;
A tailor distrustful, or partner suspicious;
A dog that is rabid, or nag that is vicious;

Above all — the chief blessings the gods can im-
　　　part, —
May you keep a clear head and a generous heart;
Remember 'tis blesséd to give and forgive;
Live chiefly to love, and love while you live;
And dying, when life's little journey is done,
May your last, fondest sigh, be PSI UPSILON!

LINES ON MY THIRTY-NINTH BIRTHDAY.

Ah me ! — the moments will not stay !
Another year has rolled away ;
And June (the second) scores the line
That tells me I am Thirty-nine !

As thus I haste the mile-stones by,
I mark the numbers with a sigh ;
And yet 't is idle to repine
I 've come so soon to Thirty-nine !

O, few that roam this world of ours,
To feel its thorns and pluck its flowers,
Have trod a brighter path than mine
From blithe thirteen to Thirty-nine !

Health, home, and friends, (life's solid part,)
A merry laugh, a fresh, young heart,

Poetic dreams, and love divine —
Have I not *these* at Thirty-nine?

O Time! — forego thy wonted spite,
And lay thy future lashes light,
And, trust me, I will not repine
At twice the count of Thirty-nine!

THINE is an ever-changing beauty; now
 With that proud look, so lofty yet serene
 In its high majesty, thou seem'st a queen,
With all her diamonds blazing on her brow!
Anon I see, — as gentler thoughts arise
 And mould thy features in their sweet control, —
 The pure, white ray that lights a maiden's soul,
And struggles outward through her drooping eyes;
Anon they flash; and now a golden light
 Bursts o'er thy beauty, like the Orient's glow,
 Bathing thy shoulders' and thy bosom's snow,
And all the woman beams upon my sight!
 I kneel unto the queen, like knight of yore;
 The maid I love; the woman I adore!

EPIGRAMS.

ON A FAMOUS WATER-SUIT.

My wonder is really boundless
    That among the queer cases we try,
A land-case should often be groundless,
    And a water-case always be dry!

KISSING CASUISTRY.

When Sarah Jane, the moral Miss,
Declares 't is very wrong to kiss,
    I'll bet a shilling I see through it;
The damsel, fairly understood,
Feels just as any Christian should, —
    She'd rather *suffer* wrong than *do* it!

THE LOST CHARACTER.

JULIA is much concerned, God wot,
For the good name — she has n't got;
So mortgagors are often known
To guard the soil they deem their own;
As if, forsooth, they did n't know
The land was forfeit long ago!

REVERSING THE FIGURES.

MARIA, just at twenty, swore
That no man less than six feet four
   Should be her chosen one.
At thirty she is glad to fix
A spouse exactly four feet six,
   As better far than none!

TO A POETICAL CORRESPONDENT.

ROSE hints she is n't one of those
Who have the gift of writing prose;
But poetry 's *une autre chose*,
And quite an easy thing to Rose!

As if an artist should decline,
For lack of skill, to paint a sign,
But, try him in the *landscape* line,
You 'll find his genius quite divine!

A DILEMMA.

" WHENEVER I marry," says masculine ANN,
" I must really insist upon wedding a *man !* "
But what if the man (for men are but human)
Should be equally nice about wedding a *woman?*

ON A LONG-WINDED ORATOR.

THREE Parts compose a proper speech,
(So wise Quintilian's maxims teach,)
But LOQUAX never can get through,
In *his* orations, more than two.
He does n't stick at the " Beginning ; "
His " Middle " comes as sure as sinning ;
Indeed, the whole one might commend,
Could he contrive to make an " *End !* "

THE THREE WIVES: A JUBILATION.

My *First* was a lady whose dominant passion
Was thorough devotion to parties and fashion;
My *Second*, regardless of conjugal duty,
Was only the worse for her wonderful beauty;
My *Third* was a vixen in temper and life,
Without one essential to make a good wife.
Jubilate! at last in my freedom I revel,
For I'm clear of the World, and the Flesh, and
     the Devil!

THE PRESS.

RECITED BEFORE THE LITERARY SOCIETIES OF BROWN UNIVERSITY, 1855.

THE PRESS.

A WORTHY parson, once upon a time,
Weary of list'ning to the sober rhyme
That, of a winter's evening, chanced to fall
From a young poet in a lecture hall,
His disappointment openly confessed,
And thus his censure to a friend confessed: —
"The poem, Sir, is well enough no doubt,
But so much preaching one could do without;
A little wit had pleased me more by half;
I did n't come to learn, I came to laugh!"

So goes the world; his very soul to save
They will not let poor Harlequin be grave;
But vote him weaker than a vestry-mouse,
Unless, like Samson, he brings down the house!

Alas! to-day, if such a rule prevail,
My sober muse were surely doomed to fail;
Her subject grave demands a serious song,
And trivial treatment were ignobly wrong. '
Yet let me hope that e'er my song be done,
When satire comes to punish with a pun,
Some pleasant fancy may your hearts beguile,
And win the favor of an answering smile.

I sing the Press; O sweet Enchantress, bring
Fit inspiration for the theme I sing,
The Art of Arts, whose earliest, freshest fame,
With fierce debate, three rival cities claim;
The glorious art, that, scorning humbler birth,
Came at a bound upon the wondering earth,[1]
Full-armed and strong her instant might to prove,
A new Minerva from the brain of Jove!

I marvel not that rival towns dispute
Where first the goddess set her radiant foot;
That blest Mayence, with honest pride, should boast
The wondrous Bible of her wizard Faust;

That Haarlem, jealous of her proper fame,
Erects a statue to her Coster's name;
While Strasburg's cits contemning all beside,
Vaunt their own hero with an equal pride.

How shall the poet venture to explain
Where plodding History labors still in vain
To solve the mystery — the vexing doubt
That only deepens with the deepening shout
Of angry partisans? The Muse essays
The dangerous task, and thus awards the bays: —
Where counter claims the highest merit hide,
If large the gift, 't is fairest to divide.
Honor to all who shared a noble part
To find, to cherish, or adorn the art;
Honor to him who, with enraptured eye,
First saw the nymph descending from the sky;
Honor to him, whate'er his name or land,
The first to kneel, and kiss her royal hand;
Thrice honored he who, piercing the disguise
That barred her beauty from obtuser eyes,
First gave her shelter, when the dusky maid
Knocked at his door in homely garb arrayed,

And found at length, beyond his hopes or prayers,
He'd wooed and won an angel unawares!

I sing the Press; alas, 't were much the same
As though the Muse essayed the trump of fame;
Though something harsh and grating in its tone,
She keeps a mightier trumpet of her own, —
The which, while Freedom's banner is unfurled,
Shall swell her pæans through the wondering world!

Strange is the sound when first the notes begin
Where human voices blend with Vulcan's din;
The click, the clank, the clangor, and the sound
Of rattling rollers in their rapid round;
The whizzing belt, the sharp metallic jar,
Like clashing spears in fierce chivalric war;
The whispering birth of myriad flying leaves,
Gathered, anon, in countless motley sheaves,
Then scattered far, as on the wingéd wind,
The mortal nurture of th' immortal mind!

I'm fond of books; 't is pleasant to behold
In various apparel, new and old,

The quaint array of well-adjusted tomes
That grace the mantels of our rural homes;
The Bible, Bunyan, Baxter, and a score
Of colder lights, from Hume to Hannah More;
Ripe with great thoughts and histories, or full
Of pious homilies, devout and dull.
Nor do I scorn those half-forgotten books
That lie neglected in obscurer nooks
Where poets mould, and critic-spiders spin
Their flimsy lines to mock the lines within!
For here the curious questioner may find
The pregnant hint that in some ampler mind
Grew to a thought, and honors now the page
That beams the brightest on the present age.

I love vast libraries; revere the fame
Of all the Ptolemies; and each other name,
Æmilius, Augustus, Crassus Cæsar, all
The old collectors, whether great or small,
Who helped the cause of learning to advance, —
Trajan and Bodley, Charles the Wise of France,
Kings, nobles, knights, who, anxious of renown
Beyond the fame of garter, spur, or crown,

And wisely provident against decay,
(Since parchment lives while marble melts away,)
Reared to their honor literary domes,
And grew immortal in immortal tomes!

Grand are the pyramids, although the stones
Are but the graves of rotten human bones
That bear, alas, nor name, nor crest, nor date
To show the world their former regal state.
Compared with these how noble and sublime
The garnered excellence of every clime
Reared in vast Pantheons, and finely wrought
From sill to cap — stone of immortal thought!

Here, e'en the sturdy democrat may find,
Nor scorn their rank, the nobles of the mind;
While kings may learn, nor blush at being shown.
How Learning's patents abrogate their own.
A goodly company and fair to see;
Royal plebeians; earls of low degree;
Beggars whose wealth enriches every clime;
Princes who scarce can boast a mental dime;
Crowd here together like the quaint array

Of jostling neighbors on a market day.
Homer and Milton — can we call them blind? —
Of godlike sight, the vision of the mind;
Shakespeare, who calmly looked creation through,
" Exhausted worlds and then imagined new;"
Plato the sage, so thoughtful and serene,
He seems a prophet by his heavenly mien;
Shrewd Socrates, whose philosophic power
Xantippe proved in many a trying hour;
And Aristophanes, whose humor run
In vain endeavor to be-"cloud" the sun;[2]
Majestic Æschylus, whose glowing page
Holds half the grandeur of the Athenian stage;
Pindar, whose odes, replete with heavenly fire,
Proclaim the master of the Grecian lyre;
Anacreon, famed for many a luscious line
Devote to Venus and the god of wine.

I love vast libraries; yet there is a doubt
If one be better with them or without, —
Unless he use them wisely, and, indeed,
Knows the high art of what and how to read;
At Learning's fountain it is sweet to drink,

But 't is a nobler privilege to think;
And oft, from books apart, the thirsting mind
May make the nectar which it cannot find.
'T is well to borrow from the good and great;
'T is wise to learn; 't is godlike to create!

There is a story which my purpose suits;
'T is told by Richter of the author *Wuz* —
A poor lone scholar who, in urgent need
(Or so he thought) of learned books to read,
Wept o'er his poverty, lamenting sore,
(The while a catalogue he pondered o'er,)
Of all the charming works that met his eye,
Not one, alas! his meagre purse could buy.
While musing thus, his racked invention brought
To weeping *Wuz* for once a lucky thought:
"Eureka!" cried the scholar, with a roar, —
As Archimedes shouted once before, —
"I have it! — True, my purse is rather scant,
But then this catalogue shows what I want,
And so who cares for poverty or pelf? —
I'll take my pen and write the books myself!"

Where be our authors now? The noble band
Dwindles apace from off the famished land.
Scarce a round dozen, at the best, remain
Of all who once, among the author-train,
Wrote books like scholars; — nor esteemed it hard,
Genius like Virtue was its own reward.

O gentle Irving! — thou whom every grace
Of wit and learning gave the highest place
In the proud synod of the old *régime*,
In all thy dreaming, didst thou ever dream
To see thy craft a mere mechanic art,
The servile minion of the bookish mart? —
When authorship should be the merest trade,
And men make books as hats and boots are made?
Didst ever dream to see the wondrous day
When the vexed press should spawn the vast array
Of trashy tomes that on the public burst,
So fast, they print the "Tenth Edition" first?
Thou hast not read them. God forbid! It racks
One's brains enough to see their brazen backs.
Yet thou wilt smile, I know, when thou art told
That with each book the buyer too is "sold";

That soon the puffing art shall all be vain,
And sense and reason rule the town again.

Sweet to the traveller is the urchin's chimes,
Proclaiming, " 'Ere's your 'Erald, Tribune, Times!"
Those lively records of the passing day,
That catch the echo, ere it dies away,
Of battle, bravery, sudden death, and all
That human minds can startle or appall;
Marriage and murder; things of different name,
Alas! that oft the two should be the same!
Letters describing merry rural scenes;
Ship-news, and, often, news for the Marines;
Fortune's bright favors, and Misfortune's shocks;
The fall of Hungary and the fall of stocks;
The important page that tells the thrilling tale
How Empires rise, and " Red Republics " fail;
How England's lion, loitering in his lair,
Essays in vain to fright the Russian bear;
How France, bemoaning the expensive war,
Would give her " Louis," to save her *louis-d'or;*
While the poor Turk, whom hapless luck attends,
Cries, " Gracious Allah! save me from my friends!"

I have a neighbor, of eccentric views,

Who has a mortal horror of the news;

As lessons are to boys, when long and hard;

Spiders, to ladies; censure, to a bard;

To losers, bets; to holders, railway stock;

Lectures to husbands, after ten o'clock;

Bacon to Hebrews, or to Quakers, war;

Squalls to a sailor, or a bachelor;

To Satan prayer-books, or to Islam, wine,

So are "the papers" to this friend of mine.

You 've but to ask him, in the common way,

The usual question, and to your dismay,

He 'll pour, remorseless, on your tingling ear,

Such streams of satire as you 'll quake to hear.

"The News? — Thank Heaven! — I 'm not the man
to know,

I do not take the papers; you can go,

If you possess the patience and the pelf,

And read the lying journals for yourself;

I hate, despise, detest, abhor them all,

Hebdomadal, diurnal, great, and small.

The *News*, indeed! — pray do you call it news

When shallow noddles publish shallow views?

Pray, is it news that turnips should be bred
As large and hollow as the owner's head?
News, that a clerk should rob his master's hoard,
Whose meagre salary scarcely pays his board?
News, that two knaves, their spurious friendship o'er,
Should tell the truths which they concealed before?
News, that a maniac, weary of his life,
Should end his sorrows with a rope or knife?
News, that a wife should violate the vows
That bind her, loveless, to a tyrant spouse?
News, that a daughter cheats paternal rule,
And weds a scoundrel to escape a fool? —
The news, indeed! — Such matters are as old
As sin and folly, rust and must and mould;
Nor fit to publish even when, in sooth,
By merest chance the papers tell the truth!"

So raves my friend, — a worthy man enough,
But in his utterance rather rude and rough;
Fond of extremes, and so exceeding strong,
E'en in the right he's often in the wrong.
One of those people whom you may have seen,
(You know them always by their nervous mien,)

Who when they go a-fishing in the well
Where Truth, the angel, is supposed to dwell,
So very roughly knock the nymph about,
She kicks the bucket ere she's fairly out!—
Yet, if they would, the noble lords of print,
E'en from my friend, might take a wholesome hint.

O for a pen with Hogarth's genius rife
To paint the scenes of Editorial life.
The tale, I know, is rather trite and old,
And yet, perchance, it may be freshly told,
As some plain dish, a simple roast or stew,
Takes a new flavor in a French *ragout.*

SCENE — a third story in a dismal court,
Where weary printers just at eight resort;
A dingy door that with a rattle shuts;
Heaps of "Exchanges," much adorned with "cuts;"
Pens, paste, and paper on the table strewed;
Books, to be read when they have been reviewed;
Pamphlets and tracts so very dull indeed
That only they who wrote them e'er will read;
Nine letters, touching themes of every sort,

And one with money — just a shilling short —
Lie scattered round upon a common level.
PERSONS — the Editor; enter, now, the Devil: —
" Please, Sir, since this 'ere article was wrote,
There 's later news perhaps you 'd like to quote: —
" The allies storming with prodigious force,
Se-*bas*-to-pol is down ! " " Set it up, of course."
" And Sir, that murder 's done — there 's only left
One larceny." " Pray don't omit the theft."
" And Sir, about the mob — the matter 's fat " —
" The mob ? — that 's wrong — pray just distribute
    that."

" And here 's an article has come to hand,
A reg'lar, 'rig'nal package " — " Let *that* stand ! "
Exit the imp of Faust, and enter now
A fierce subscriber with a scowling brow ; —
" Sir, curse your paper ! — send the thing to " —
    Well,
The place he names were impolite to tell ;
Enough to know the hero of the Press
Cries, " Thomas, change the gentleman's address !
We 'll send the paper, if the post will let it,
Where the subscriber will be sure to get it ! "

Who would not be an Editor? — To write
The magic "we" of such enormous might;
To be so great beyond the common span
It takes the plural to express the man;
And yet, alas, it happens oftentimes
A unit serves to number all his dimes!

But don't despise him; there may chance to be
An earthquake lurking in his simple "we!"
   In the close precincts of a dusty room
That owes few losses to the lazy broom,
There sits the man; you do not know his name,
Brown, Jones, or Johnson — it is all the same —
Scribbling away at what perchance may seem
An idler's musing, or a dreamer's dream;
His pen runs rambling, like a straying steed;
The "we" he writes seems very "wee" indeed;
But mark the change; behold the wondrous power
Wrought by the Press in one eventful hour;
To-night, 't is harmless as a maiden's rhymes;
To-morrow, thunder in the *London Times!*
The ministry dissolves that held for years;
Her Grace, the Duchess, is dissolved in tears;

The   Rothschilds   quail ;   the   church,   the   army,
    quakes ;
The   very   kingdom   to   its   centre   shakes ;
The   Corn   Laws   fall ;   the   price   of   bread   comes
    down —
Thanks   to   the   " we "   of   Johnson,   Jones,   or   Brown !

Firm   in   the   right,   the   daily   Press   should   be
The   tyrant's   foe,   the   champion   of   the   free ;
Faithful   and   constant   to   its   sacred   trust ;
Calm   in   its   utterance ;   in   its   judgments,   just ;
Wise   in   its   teaching ;   uncorrupt,   and   strong
To   speed   the   right,   and   to   denounce   the   wrong.
Long   may   it   be   ere   candor   must   confess
On   Freedom's   shores   a   weak   and   venal   Press.